TOWER OF
DREAMS

TOWER OF DREAMS

Kathryn K. Abdul-Baki

LYNNE
RIENNER
PUBLISHERS

BOULDER
LONDON

A Three Continents Book

Cover painting by Nabila Hilmi. Cover design by Judy Smith.

Published in the United States of America in 2003 by
Lynne Rienner Publishers, Inc.
1800 30th Street, Boulder, Colorado 80301
www.rienner.com

and in the United Kingdom by
Lynne Rienner Publishers, Inc.
3 Henrietta Street, Covent Garden, London WC2E 8LU

ISBN 0-89410-817-4 (pbk. : alk. paper)

Printed and bound in the United States of America

ACKNOWLEDGEMENTS

Portions of this novel appeared earlier and in somewhat different form as stories, "Hala" and "Kuwait 1956", in *Union Street Review* and in *Fields of Fig and Olive: Ameera and Other Stories of the Middle East.*

THANKS

To all members of my family for their love and support, to Dr. Donald Herdeck for his sensitive and insightful editing and to Ellen Stone for her generous help with earlier versions of the manuscript.

DEDICATION

To the memories of my mother, Jean, my grandmother, Helen, and my cousin, Nora, who live on in my heart.

And to Kuwait, as I knew it.

Contents

PROLOGUE

A sky charred by myriad blazing fires, a desert sun dimmed by sheets of black smoke, and an aqua sea floating—as though in mourning—beneath a film of black oil. Oil, the very sustenance of the land, the magnet that drew us all to the desert to begin with, now threatening to destroy all.

These new images, like the gaping war craters left on the silken desert plain, assault the memories of an earlier, placid calm: cloudless sleepy skies, the ripple of heat against sand, a nomad's dark tent beside a gleaming car, a sea cucumber washed ashore on a limpid wave. Then, come the old dreams, dreams of promised riches, of love, of a happiness that we never doubted would be ours.

We were like sisters then, Laila and I, childhood friends loving each other and hating each other, never once imagining that we would not always be together. It never occurred to me, then, that there would be no way to bring it all back—not Laila, not the old Kuwait before the disappointments set in, not the dreams before they dried up. Even after I met *him*, when I discovered the puzzling, furious love between a man and a woman, the love that locks out all else, I continued to love Laila. She was sealed in my heart like the remembrance of the desert as it was when we first arrived, pure and boundless and

1

promising. For in those days, I believed that we would be there for each other forever—in that maternal desert by the sea.

I never told Laila this. . .

ISABEL, 1956

@ time a monarchy?
now libral democracy.

1

I am ready to go, in a hurry because soon Laila will arrive in her new car, a blazing red MG. It is due to her daring—I almost say wantonness but that would be unfair considering that she is doing this for me—that I am, tonight, about to present myself to Saqr.

For three years, ever since I was fourteen, Saqr has waited for me. And I have dreamed of this moment, dreamed of blooming at his touch like a desert dandelion after rain, desiring him as fiercely as he has me—all in secret, of course, for I would never tell him so.

Now, as I study my face one last time in the mirror, pale foundation hiding my freckles, kohl and black mascara veiling green eyes, peach lipstick, I bid good-bye to the face of the child, already missing it, knowing that when I come home, I will see a stranger.

"One spade."

"Two hearts."

"Two diamonds."

Light laughter comes from the other room, then a man's reprimand—my father's impatience with my mother's low bidding. They are playing bridge in the dining room with the neighbors. Although they have given me permission to spend the evening at a friend's house, they are wary of Laila, only seventeen, driving me there.

I peer out of the window but see no MG yet—only the lights stretching like a strand of pearls across the desert to the compound's club in the distance where people will be sitting outdoors watching one of the weekly English movies as they nurse cold drinks to drown the heat. Inside my bedroom, my desk is immaculate now that school is over. The dresser top is strewn with jars of creams and cosmetics instead of books. My favorite doll—a straw Baluchistan princess with many skirts, bought on a childhood trip with my mother to Iran—perches in the middle. I look in the mirror again, stare at those deceiving eyes. Then I start on my hair.

The comb stops midway through, trapped in a nest of tangles made worse by the humidity and years of brackish water. My red hair grows, expands, fluffs coarsely in the dampness, untamed by any brush or comb so that I have to work gently from the bottom up, one small barb at a time, to free the strands. I suddenly remember that other time, nearly eleven years ago, when a painful twinge at my scalp signaled the beginning of a new world.

I was six years old and sitting beside my mother in an airplane, searching out the window for the giant sandbox my father had promised me. We were flying to the Arabian Gulf from New York, after an hour's transit in Cairo. To make the move away from our green suburban neighborhood and my friends in New York more tolerable, my father promised me the biggest sandbox I had ever seen. I looked for it now, scanning the endless beige ridges thousands of feet below the plane, hoping to sight the little wooden-framed sandbox like the one in my school back in White Plains.

Kuwait. I said the strange word over to myself just as my father taught me. Kuwait was the name of our new home. It meant 'little fort', my father said.

Again, I felt the pulling at my scalp. I whipped around but was not quick enough to catch it. I looked up at my mother, but she only smiled at me benevolently, above it all. I took another quick glance behind me through the crack between our seats, the same crack that the thing had passed through to grab my hair.

The thing turned out to be a hand, although at first it seemed like a claw the way the thin fingertips were tinted orange and the brown skin was wrinkled and dry. Behind me, in a previously empty seat, sat midnight. Black-rimmed eyes were surrounded by a black, satiny mask and further dimmed by a gold-flecked black veil. A black cloak held securely at the chin covered the hair and body.

"Is it Zorro?" I asked my mother.

Twice, so far, the fancy Zorro had reached between my mother's seat and mine and pulled at my hair. Twice, my mother whispered to me not to worry, that it was only because my hair was red, and the woman had probably never seen red hair before, that she wanted to check to see if it was real.

My mother was American, with hair even redder than mine and eyes that were a watery blue. My Arab father had rich, brown eyes and black hair. I looked like my mother but my eyes were green. For a long time, because of my mother's blue eyes and my father's brown ones, I assumed that blue and brown made green.

"Give her a jelly bean," my mother said, nodding to the paper bag of candy in my lap that we bought in New York just before boarding. I looked at my mother, despairing at the calm she could muster in this situation. I did not want to give up my

7

jelly beans, certainly not to the night rider behind me.

"Give her one, Isabel," my mother insisted.

Reluctantly, I turned around and pushed the bag part-way through our seats. I saw, through the woman's veil, her eyes darting from my face to the bag and back. As I waited, her orange fingers emerged, almost shyly, from within the silken, black folds. She leaned forward a bit and through the gold and black of her veil, her wide, pretty eyes seemed to dance with pleasure as she reached into the bag and retrieved a red jelly bean.

I turned away, glad to have that over, hoping the candy would keep her occupied while I resumed my search from the window for the long-awaited sandbox.

2

The desert was hotter than anyone could imagine. The first few days were an endless sandstorm, a *toz* the Arabs called it, tiny needles flaying my arms and face and enveloping the entire landscape in a beige cloud. When the air settled, the August sun scorched whatever grass and trees were spared by the storm. I believed it when several British and American women, the expatriate wives of employees of the oil company my father now worked for, told my mother that the concrete got hot enough to fry an egg. It fried the soles of my feet when I stepped outside the front door to contemplate the endless dunes, the flat, disappointing sandbox that my father promised. I never quite forgave him for tricking me, nor had I forgiven my mother for going along with his joke and for smiling when my father confessed that this was it—the *desert* was the sandbox. It was as though it had not occurred to them that what I really wanted was a simple wooden sandbox with just enough sand for making pies and tunnels. The desert was more sand than I could fathom. What would I do with it all? Where would I begin?

Our house was in a sprawling residential compound built right on the shore of the Arabian Gulf and not far from the oil refinery, itself. With its ever-burning flare high atop a long pipe, the refinery was a constant reminder of why we were in Kuwait. The compound, surrounded by a high, barbed-wire fence and protected from trespassers by a guard at the main gate by the refinery, had been built expressly for the families of the company's expatriate employees. The modern, air-conditioned homes had been completely, and identically, furnished from the United States and once inside any of them, the grim, Arab desert could be forgotten for a while. Except, that is, for when a *toz* would hit. Then it was as though the desert would reassert itself once more, the sand seeping into the houses through the cracks beneath the doors and between the window panes, settling in the air like fairy dust, coating the furniture and the clothing hung inside the closets with a milky film. Even the towels placed under doors and against windows could not prevent this sand-seepage, as if the desert could penetrate the very walls if it so chose!

There was a club within walking distance of our house which had a restaurant, a library, and a movie theater which showed films several times a week. Since there was no television station in Kuwait yet, and since we had no telephones in this remote part of the desert, the club provided a necessary social outlet for adults and children alike. Along with the sea several hundred yards away, a smooth, glittering carpet of diamonds in the morning, deep and dark green during the day, and mauve in the evening at low tide when the water drew back so far it seemed to have been sucked into the horizon, the club was the only other respite that summer from the infinite days of heat and boredom.

There was little time to worry, however, because school would be starting in September.

10

There were no English schools in the desert except for a small correspondence school run for the children of expatriate employees. My mother, with characteristic bravado, enrolled me in both that school and in the Arab girls' public school in Shuaiba, a fishing village three miles up the coast, both so that I might learn Arabic and have the benefit of a 'real' school.

On my first day there, I was put in the care of a tall girl with a black ponytail tied with white elastic and protruding breasts under her green-checked uniform, who paraded me about the school, showing me off to her friends, to the teachers, to the two cleaning women wearing gauzy pantaloons and white veils. All the while, she smiled at me and fed me cookies from a box of glazed animal crackers.

"I won't go there any more. They speak only Arabic," I cried to my mother when I got home, half sick from the heat.

"Well, you'd better learn quickly or you're going to feel stupid," my mother said, standing at the stove, frying chicken.

I stared at her back, shocked that she would actually contemplate sending me back to that frightening place where there were only a handful of fair-skinned girls and where I was the only redhead.

The image I retained of my mother during those years was that adamant expanse of her back while she was cooking, while she was kneeling in the sun to coax petunias and zinnias from the stubborn sand, while she drifted about her bedroom in nothing but perfume and jewelry as she dressed to go out to a party. Sometimes, that body—the small, dainty breasts, the long neck—inspired me with love. I, too, wanted to have cupcake breasts that swung when I moved, and a twisting chignon that would display my neck. Other times, such as when she quietly went on with her cooking instead of reassuring me that I would never, ever, have to return to the school in Shuaiba, this same body made me angry, as though it had suddenly turned overly ripe and ungainly.

11

Later, when she got into her bed for her usual afternoon read and a nap, I crawled in beside her.

"Tell me a story," I said.

"Now?" She said, though she put down her book on the stack of paperbacks on the bedside table.

"Make one up," I said, closing my eyes.

"I'm so sleepy," she said, snuggling further into the blanket, "so it'll be just a short one. A short, short one."

I knew that her mind was already racing, painting the lush habitat for the characters that peopled her stories. Of course, the main character was always some little girl named Isabel.

"Once upon a time, Uncle paid a visit to Isabel," she began.

"Why?" I asked, already breathless.

"Because," my mother said, mysteriously, "Uncle was setting out on a very important adventure in Shuaiba, and he needed Isabel's help..."

These moments between my mother and I were to become routine in Kuwait. To my delight, she began to take naps regularly, sleeping away the dry, hot afternoons much like the Kuwaitis, Pakistanis, Indians, Iranians, and other Arabs although since we had air-conditioning we had no real cause for fatigue. Perhaps it was the water, never quite free of the sea from which it came, that brought on this drowsiness. Perhaps it was the presence of competent house boys to do the household chores that allowed for more time to relax. Perhaps it was, simply, the fact that aside from going to the beach, attending the occasional women's luncheon or tea, or overseeing the general needs of the house, there was not much else to do.

12

3

Despite my balking, I returned to the Arabic school the next day and the next. After the third week, the school was moved from the dilapidated, gypsum structure with crumbling wind towers to a bright, new pink and turquoise cement building with latticed balconies that overlooked the sea. It was the most beautiful building I had ever seen. Beyond the playground, aqua, yellow, azure, mauve, and yellow again at the sandbars were the colors of the Gulf. The brilliance of the water as it echoed the harsh sun was enough to sear the eyes. In this new, and more attractive, setting I began to adjust.

Sea gulls circled above the playground in the mornings before the bell rang as groups of girls walked arm-in-arm, memorizing the day's lessons while others played hopscotch in the sand, flicking a flat rock from square to square with their toes. I usually joined in a game of 'wolf and mother' where a train of girls, led by a 'mother' chanted, "I am the mother who will

13

protect you," to an opposing train led by a 'wolf' who retorted, "I am the wolf who will eat you!" The object was for the 'wolves' to grab as many girls as they could from the 'mother', thus turning the 'children' into 'wolves', themselves.

During break, we would gaze over the low school wall at the waves slapping the shore, the translucent water turning into a murky froth of shells, sand, and bubbles as it broke. Girls were not allowed in the water and did not swim. Only the boys from the school next door were permitted to strip down to their black trunks and hurl themselves, oblivious, into the waves as the girls watched, shouting in fear and envy.

At lunch time we sat at long tables as Omar, the broad-bellied cook, ladled yellow lentil soup into our mugs. One of the cleaning women, Hassa, who wore a heavy silver ring in her nose, passed out hard-boiled eggs and cheese sandwiches.

It was at lunch that I first noticed Laila. Laila S. I remembered her from class, a girl with milk-white skin and black, marble eyes. *Laila*: Night. I was intimidated from the start by the girl who smirked rather than smiled, by her flashing eyes and black, unruly pigtails, by her taunting pink lips.

She stared at me. "I am Lebanese," she said, fearlessly, announcing that she, too, was different, not like the others, at the same time pushing away her plate with the egg and sandwich untouched.

Weeks passed and the new school routine took over. I started each morning at the Arabic school. When the bell rang, we lined up two-by-two, according to class, to do arm exercises and jumping-jacks, sing the national anthem, and lower our heads to recite the Muslim *Fatiha*. Afterwards came inspection time. Each girl would stand in her crisply-pressed uniform and starched hair ribbon—the work of Shuaiba's pressing shop since

14

most of the village's modest homes had few electrical appliances—then pull out a folded handkerchief to hold in her orange, hennaed hands as a sort of backdrop to display her clean, short nails.

If it was a Monday, hair was checked for lice. Using two pencils so as not to soil their hands, the teachers poked through each girl's scented, oiled hair in search of the offending parasites. The obviously well-scrubbed girls, such as Laila and myself, were often passed by. Others were doubly-scrutinized and sometimes led away, first for a haircut, then to sit, sobbing, in a corner of the bathroom while their hair was fumigated with DDT and their heads wrapped in nets.

School ended at one o'clock, ten minutes before the boys' school next door so that the girls could get home without mingling with the boys along the way. Girls who were seen dawdling in the road were sharply reprimanded by the teachers the next morning. I was the only one allowed to remain at the gate after school since I waited for our driver who came in a white car to take me back to our compound.

Sometimes, though, the driver was late, and I was still standing at the gate when the boys were let out. With their heavy satchels and gray uniform jackets, their hair shaved to a bristle, they looked like small soldiers. They stared at me as they passed, at my red hair, my freckles and green eyes. They would smile, baring crooked yellowed teeth, and call out, "*Quitta*! Cat! Meow!"

From the lively Shuaiba school, where the hot, open- windowed rooms were cooled by whirring ceiling fans, where girls walked down the halls or in the playground arm-in-arm, where the air carried both the smells of saffron and lentils from the kitchen and the scent of coconut oil and henna from the girls' hair, I was driven back to the compound's English school. Here, I sat in a frigid, air-conditioned room for another two hours of work in English with the expatriate children. We were fifteen

15

girls and boys, ranging from first to seventh graders, in a room of a building originally built as a commissary. We worked individually, under the guidance of an English woman named Mrs. Potter, who sent off our monthly exams to be graded by an assigned but faceless teacher in London or Baltimore, depending on whether one was following the British or the American curriculum. Because I only attended half-day, I remained something of an outsider to my expatriate classmates. Once, one of the girls, Andrea Deer, poured fruit juice all over my books inside my desk.

I usually arrived at the English school just in time for the midday break and a game of "farmer in the dell" or "Red Rover." When we were a little older, it was often a heady game of "spin the bottle." Of course, I never mentioned to the girls in Shuaiba that I participated in something as unthinkable and vile as kissing some strange boy if the bottle pointed at one.

Those first few weeks and months in the desert and in my new school were marked by two lingering images.

The first was the memory of our garden clothesline forever strung with brownish shirts and underwear—men's, ladies', and children's white shirts and panties tinted the brown of the brackish water forced out of the shriveled earth. All the houses in the compound looked much the same from the backyards.

The other image was that of the glistening, honey color of the locusts, the *jaraad* that besieged us that September. To those living in an expatriate compound intent on bringing some semblance of Western culture into the inhospitable desert, the locusts came as a sudden, unwelcome sight. My mother and I dashed about our patio clanging kitchen pans to scatter the horde that descended hungrily on our new trees and on the patches of soil that my mother was determined to turn into flower beds. Still, by the end of the day, the zinnias were gone, and the oleander and frangipani leaves were whittled to stubs.

16

The Kuwaitis, however, like other desert peoples who had faced this scourge countless times before, dealt with the pests in a different manner. In school the following day, there was cause for a celebration. Fried up crisp and golden, the wings and legs removed, the locusts were brought from home in jars or oily paper bags for the mid-day snack. With mouth-watering abandon, girls dangled the delicacies into their mouths. I shrank from an invitation to taste and was nauseated the next few weeks as school seemed to take on the locusts' moist, amber hue as they were sneaked out of desks to be shared between classes, just as the teachers' heels could be heard rounding the corner.

LAILA

4

There was an uncle in the family, my father's older brother, Issa, who was an innocent sort. Nobody in our village of *Zahle*, in Lebanon, ever had the heart to come right out and say that he was crazy although they all knew it, just as they knew that he had two main pastimes—weddings and funerals.

Both weddings and funerals involved a good deal of eating for those who took part in the processions—even when they were dismal—and Uncle Issa would string along at the end of the impassioned crowd making its way through the village in eager anticipation of this.

It was not that my uncle was ill fed at home. His wife, despite her quick temper, was never stingy and spent most of her day preparing elaborate meals for her three children and stout Issa. However, my uncle's mind had gone limp to the point that he seemed to want immediate gratification of whatever need presented itself to him at the moment. If he was hungry and he happened by a crowd, he would lumber along foolishly, patiently, knowing that the end result was bound to be a feast.

Frequenting the village streets more than his home, Issa would be lost for days before being found in the most unpredictable spots—slumped along a wall in the shade of some balcony, his tongue stretched out to catch the drops of water trickling down from a pot of just-watered geraniums, bent over onto his knees with his face in the dust, whispering to himself as he worshiped the sun. Usually it was my father who found him and returned him home to his wife.

My aunt would scream at Uncle Issa and tuck him into bed, only to find him risen and gone again later. Toward the end, Uncle Issa claimed that the village square was the only place in which to find peace. Day after day he would sit there to watch the sun rise. There my father found him one morning, dead of a heart attack at the age of thirty-five.

I never knew Uncle Issa. I only knew that he was responsible for our leaving the pretty mountain village in Lebanon and moving to the desert. Far away from the white stone houses with red roofs and flowers sprouting from every window and balcony, far from the carts stacked with peaches and green apples the size of melons, far from the terraced orchards across the valley and the crisp morning air that slapped our faces when we opened the windows, far from all that he loved, my father believed that he could forget his older brother once and for all. Maybe he thought that putting such distance between him and his roots would sever the possibility of his inheriting his brother's illness.

Sometime during the summer that I turned six, we arrived on this spot of sand so hot and vast and probably invisible to the rest of humanity. We arrived in Kuwait.

The 'we' who arrived from our lush Zahle were myself, my mother, my father, my older brother, and my barrel of a grandmother who always smelled—no matter how frequently she washed—of sweet, rotting pears.

Only weeks before, this fleshy, wrinkled old woman whose white hair crawled below her back in a curved braid, this woman who could cajole me into her arms with a croon or terrorize me with a single pout, was the woman I believed to be my own mother. I even called her 'Mama'.

She was the woman who had appeared before me ever since I could remember, the woman whose presence filled my every waking hour and my turbulent dreams, who had fed me with her fingers bread and salt when there was nothing in the house to eat, who had bathed me in the metal tub of water in which she had just washed our clothes when water was scarce, who rubbed my body with oil and salt to make my bones strong. She was fearless, once catching a mouse with her bare hand as it scurried up a curtain. I wanted to be just like her—strong, harsh, and brave.

How did I learn that this woman whom I both feared and adored was not, in fact, my mother?

One day, Aida, the pretty young woman I thought of as my cousin, came to the house. She had waves of chestnut hair and skin as pure and white as the fresh cream my grandmother skimmed off the top of my boiled milk each morning. I liked the way she smelled, deep, aromatic, and mysterious. After giving me her usual loving kiss and pinch on my cheek, she told my grandmother to start packing because we were all leaving.

I stared at this pretty young woman of whom I was usually so fond. Leaving? How could we leave Zahle?

Of course my grandmother argued with Aida. As a rule, she resisted anyone telling her what to do. I stood on a stool in the kitchen listening to the women and gazing through the purple vine outside the window at a man who leaned against our garden wall. He wore a crisp suit and smoked a cigarette, and I was sure that I recognized him as the brother of crazy Issa, the village dimwit.

That night, my grandmother rocked me to sleep against her breast, telling me that we had to leave our home and go with Aida. She explained that it was Aida—not she—who was my mother. The man who had waited outside was Aida's husband, the man who should have been my father but was not.

She told me the truth that night—that I was not the child of my mother's husband even though I should have been since they were married long before I was born and even had a son, Sameer, who was my older brother. That she told me this so bluntly did not surprise me. My grandmother was neither delicate nor indulgent and did not spare me the detail that I was Aida's bastard daughter. Yet I held her no grudge for this. Although her methods of showing it were occasionally extreme, she was utterly devoted to me, and she made sure that I knew it.

So, I was a bastard. This was shocking, yet, in a strange way, exciting news. I was different, special in an odd way. Not that I comprehended the extent of this shame or its further implications on my life. At six, I only knew that something drastic had changed my life.

Gone was the cozy polarity between me and the old woman. Instead, an entirely new galaxy appeared on the horizon consisting of a mother, a father/stepfather, and an older brother— the last whom I did not know nor want to. It was thrust upon me like a piece of broken glass, this new family, and I was supposed to absorb each and every member of it into myself, just like that. Yet like broken glass in a wound, each time I thought I had accepted this fact, it seemed to ooze back out of me, alien, rejected by my very being.

The reason for this sudden revelation, my grandmother explained, was that my new father/stepfather was moving us all away to another country where he would make enough money for us to live like kings.

The fact that my grandmother was being hauled off along with me was the only, albeit small, consolation in the face of this sudden, terrifying news.

24

5

Our first few days in the dusty, damp city of Kuwait were so blistering that only my father ventured outside. I smelled the wetness in the air and felt the heat that made me want to tear off my clothes simply in order to breath. Having lived only in the cool of mountains, none of us had confronted humidity before.

I was sick and drowsy those first few days, my discomfort compounded by my worrying that I was not presenting myself in a favorable light to my new family. We were staying in the crowded apartment of relatives who had agreed to put up my father before they knew that he was bringing along a wife, two children, and a mother-in-law.

Unfortunately, Aida quickly grew grumpy when she realized that the full rewards of our uprooting were not going to materialize as quickly as she had imagined. For the time being, squeezed into a bedroom with her husband, son, mother, and sick daughter, she had to help out with the cleaning, cooking, and caring for the several small children of our hosts. I overheard her grumble to my grandmother more than once that she had not given up her own daughter all these years to run after someone else's brat, while my father suffered the hundred-degree heat to find a job.

The few times I ventured out of the apartment building with my grandmother in late afternoons did not allay my fears. Construction was everywhere. Cinder blocks were piled carelessly as though a child had stacked them, rickety planks of wood bridged gaping holes, and tunnels were being dug by dark men in ragged turbans and reddish smocks the colors of the distant sunset. Gone were the brilliant, white-stone houses of Zahle. In their place were ugly, unpainted concrete walls or the older mud-brick houses which seemed about to disintegrate at a mere touch. There was an unsettling, transient look about the place that suggested that it might all be gone tomorrow, gulped back down into the deep sand.

I recognized only a few familiar words of Arabic around us while the rest was gibberish: Urdu, Hindi, Farsi, Swahili used by the workers—Pakistanis, Indians, Baluchis, Somalis—who, like us, I would later learn, had come in search of a new life.

The indigenous men of Kuwait strode about in long, white *dishdashas* and sheer, white headdresses which were held in place by a black cord or else folded back as one would a towel over wet hair. Women, enveloped in silky, billowing black *abayas* seemed to glide down the street as though on silent wheels.

Finally, we got lucky. By the end of the third week, my father found a job as a welder for an oil company and with it came a small house several miles from the refinery in a village by the sea. With our belongings strapped to the top of a taxi, we rode out of the baking city along a lone black road into the boundless desert. The ride seemed interminable. We might have driven all the way back to Lebanon! The only signs of life were the occasional black tents of bedouins and their few goats. When it seemed that we could drive no further, that we would be marooned and swallowed up by the blank, soft sand, I saw it. We all saw it—a thin ribbon across the horizon in the distance just above the car's hood.

I stretched up to glimpse better what everyone else seemed so excited about. It was barely discernible from the cloudless sky—yet it was a darker, richer blue than the sky, quickly growing into another vast space. It was water. The sea. We had reached the village by the sea. We had reached our new home—*Shuaiba*.

6

We settled in quickly. Our small house was surrounded by a maze of narrow lanes with high, mud walls that were punctured by occasional doors. Some of these doors were of dark wood and were so short that it seemed they had been made expressly for children. Other doors were large and carved in minute detail with zigzags, arabesques, and even flowers. Ours was a plain door of blue-painted wood that seemed to relieve the intense heat that reigned throughout, as though one had come upon a dazzling lake.

Several days later, I ventured into the road to face whatever might be of interest. There were other girls in the alley—slender, copper-skinned, with eyes as wide and dark as plums. A few, about my age, would suddenly pop out of one of the doors in the walls to run to the market or carry a baby about for a walk. Some of the girls wore the blousy, black sheets of the women over their long dresses, often with long, embroidered white pants underneath. Some even came up and spoke to me in their strange dialect, but most of them simply stared.

Soon, though, word must have spread that there was a new girl about, for entire bunches of girls began to stroll into our alley where I spent a lot of time in front of our door to make myself available for questions such as where did I come from, and what was a mountain, and was there really such a thing as snow? In time, we became friends and I spent the last weeks of summer mostly in the road outside our blue door playing hop-scotch and tag.

Among the Shuaiba girls I now set a standard. They began to think me sophisticated with my strange accent and my knowl-edge of places other than their flat desert. Often the older girls would say, "Wait for Laila," if there was something of interest about to take place.

Even my new family seemed less alien, now. My grandmother seemed reconciled to relinquish control over family matters to Aida, and my step-father, in a special effort to be friendly, taught me to play backgammon and cards after supper. Were it not for Sameer, I might have soon become as happy in Shuaiba as I had been in Zahle.

It was strange having a big brother. Sometimes Sameer seemed to be cruel, screaming at me for no reason, even spitting at me if I did something that displeased him. Other times he was protective and even kind, allowing me to play with wire cars that he fashioned for himself to play with in the streets with the other boys. I mostly ignored Sameer, however, and he was just older and taller enough than I not to have to pay me too much attention. Yet, this brother, the true child of my mother and her husband, must have resented me. Aida frequently sent him to buy me cookies and the pink, coconut candy I loved from the Shuaiba market since I was a girl and too young, she felt, to be let loose in the alien streets. At night, when it was time to wash for bed, Aida washed my feet in the pail before Sameer's so that I always had the fresh water. Although ambivalent about him, I was not too concerned by Sameer's treatment of me,

29

since he was equally caustic to Aida and barely acknowledged my grandmother. In fact, I soon realized that the only person who could hold Sameer's respect, if indeed his sullen silence could be called that, was his father.

Birth always brought death. That was what my grandmother said one morning although, at the time, she could not have known whose death she was predicting.

She was reading Aida's coffee cup, the two of them pausing in the morning chore of sweeping and rinsing the courtyard to each drink a small cup of orange-blossom flavored coffee. With dresses tied above their knees, they sat on stools in the shade while I secretly watched them from inside the house, jealous, sensing that it was a private moment for them. More and more, I had begun to notice both my grandmother and Aida enjoying the renewed comradeship between them which had been lacking over the past years due to my presence and to Aida's need to separate herself from me.

They sat among the large tins of oleanders and jasmine bushes, cooling their bare feet in the water they had just sloshed onto the ground, momentarily oblivious to the morning heat. It was as hard for me to believe that my stern, ungainly grandmother had begotten the beautiful younger woman beside her as it was for me to believe that Aida had begotten me—or Sameer, for that matter. Ladies as young and alluring as Aida were not mothers.

Except for the shared milky complexion, the two women seemed as different from one another as the sun from the moon, as a pomegranate from honey. While my grandmother scorched and stung in her own loving way, Aida glowed sweetly, especially around me. I could tell that she was eager to make up for the lost years when we lived apart by indulging me with kisses and sweets.

However, it was the shared moment between this other mother

and daughter that I observed the morning that my grandmother saw in Aida's cup that she was pregnant and then immediately followed that with the pronouncement that a death was imminent.

I wandered out into the courtyard.

"What do you think of that?" Aida said, smiling up at me, obviously wondering whether I had overheard about her pregnancy.

"Who's going to die?" I said, ignoring her.

"Nobody's going to die. Your mother's going to have a baby," my grandmother said, clearing her throat and spitting onto the ground.

"I heard you say that a birth brings a death."

They both stood up. Aida opened her arms to me but I fled into the arms of my grandmother. Before, she would have explained to me what she meant right then and there, honestly and without reservation. With my mother present, however, the old woman was no longer as open with me. She had someone else now, someone older and more interesting, to confide in.

I nursed a pang of hatred for Aida, wishing that all of her glossy brown curls would fall out and that she would blow up so big with her new baby that she would explode and die. Deep within me, I knew that the only person around me who was old enough to die was my grandmother, and I was not about to let anyone, especially not Aida's new baby, take her away from me. I soon rejected this idea, however. It had to be somebody else. Maybe Sameer would die.

Several days later, after my grandmother's prophecy of death, I did something wrong, something which involved lying or stealing or both. Perhaps I took some loose change from my new father's trouser pocket and then denied it. Whatever the childish misdeed, my grandmother was going to settle the matter her own way. For although she, for the most part, had surrendered both herself and me up to my parents to feed, clothe, and take care of, she did not believe that anyone but herself was fit to discipline me. Sameer, at eight, was far too indulged as far as she was concerned, running off into the streets with strange boys he barely knew, never around whenever she or Aida needed something from the market or from the pressing shop. She was not about to allow me be so ruined.

Now, my grandmother had punished me for lying once before—a long time ago in Zahle. Knowing what was in store, I decided not to submit to it again.

When she came looking for me after Aida left the house to visit some neighbor, I hid behind the dining room door. Through the crack, I could see the reddened tip of the meat skewer sensing its way through the air toward me. For my grandmother's remedy for lying was to sear the tops of the knuckles of both of my hands—ten scars to ward away the ten evil *jinns* who had taught me to lie!

Of course that hurt, although not as much as I led her to imagine, but I still had ten small scars on my knuckles from the last time, ten dots that blanched whiter than the rest of my skin, and I did not want ten more. I especially did not want to be humiliated before my new family now that I was just finding my proper place among them, especially not before Sameer, who I thought would enjoy seeing me punished.

As Grandmother searched one room, I quickly sneaked into the next one, once her back was turned. Although not the stronger one, I was certainly the lighter, without her girth and faded hearing. By the time she reached the dining room I was under the bed in Aida's room, safe and dusty against the cool tile.

All at once she screamed my name: "Laila!"

It was such a rasping, horrible cry, that I nearly crawled out from my hiding place to deliver myself to her rather than hear that strange, growling noise again. But I stayed still, hoping she would give up and go away.

All at once, there was a loud thud and the clinking of metal against stone. I froze in my spot, afraid to move or look out. I knew she had fallen, for I heard the sound of the skewer dropping onto the floor. The whole house seemed to shake and ring, each sound separate, dissected in my mind. Yet I could not move. Even though I suddenly envisioned her dying, even though I wanted one last look at her while she still lived, I lay still, paralyzed.

The dust tickled my nose. I waited for one more sound, a stirring to indicate that she had merely stumbled, but there was only the sound of my own breathing, the distant echo of voices in the streets mingled with the cry of noon prayers from the mosque down the road.

Aida returned and found her mother sprawled on the dining room floor, eyes wide, arms rigid as the steel skewer in her hand. She began to scream to the neighbors, to God, to Sameer, for help (she repeated this over and over to us afterwards as though it would rid the image from her memory).

Finally, someone found my father. When he got home to a house full of alarmed neighbors and a draped body on his dining room floor, his only words were: "Where is Laila?"

Still under the bed, terrified by Aida's howling and too stunned to reveal myself, I waited while they searched.

I had killed her! She had crumpled in anger. Now, surely, they would kill me.

I held my breath, hoping to suffocate like my grandmother, to be put out of the confused misery of this new life. However, my grandmother had predicted only one death. Obviously, it was not mine.

It did not take long for someone to look under the bed and to coax me out, but it was my father who lifted me into his arms. Hot, dusty, and crying, I lay my aching head against his shoulder, rubbing my face against his shirt until my nose stopped itching.

"Poor one, poor little Laila," he kept murmuring, never minding that his white shirt was becoming gray beneath my face, as though he knew exactly what had happened.

Even Sameer tried to comfort me. He lay down on my bed and said that I could hold onto him if I wanted. Aida sent him away and let me touch her belly, instead, reminding me that we were a family, that a new child was coming.

We cried together a while, Aida for the mother she had just come to know again in a new way, I for my very life, for the future of the entire universe. For with Grandmother gone, surely nothing and no one was safe anymore.

Aida pulled me close to her and told me that I was young, that my life was just beginning. I would be starting school soon in Shuaiba and would be too busy to be sad.

I said that I was unhappy and wanted to go back to Lebanon. That is when she told me that we would never go back.

"It's because of Issa. Your father wants to forget Issa," she said. Then she sighed and wiped her hands over her face as though to protect herself from some curse. "Sometimes I think Sameer is a little like Issa. But maybe not."

Lying there, I thought of Issa, my father's older brother who had died so miserably so long ago.

"We are not going back to Lebanon," Aida repeated, the night that Grandmother died. "Soon you'll be in school. And think of the friends you have already. Why look back?"

I nodded. I did have new friends in Shuaiba.

"I only wish that Sameer had more friends," Aida said. He's not exactly like Issa, but he isn't like you. Everyone on this street knows Laila."

I smiled, knowing that what she said was true. Everyone in our alley knew me. I had made friends. Unlike Sameer.

I never knew whether or not I had killed my grandmother. Perhaps it was the job of raising a child at her age that sent her off. For months afterward I felt her presence around me, as if she were swallowed up by the house and yet still in it.

I knew that her spirit was with us for the forty days following

34

her death—that she walked these rooms, sat with us at meal-time, and lay down to sleep right along with the rest of us. Even though I never spoke about her to anyone, not even to Aida, I knew that she was present. It was almost as if she had burrowed into me.

For instance, I began to crave onions. She had loved onions, herself, and used to add them to almost anything she cooked. She would chop and then fry them, turning them into tiny pearls, teardrops, in the hot oil before adding them to rice or meat. As though her addiction to onions had been transferred to me, I specifically asked Aida to put them into anything I ate.

Then, of course, there was her peculiar smell of decomposing fruit that lingered about the house. Once she was gone, the smell grew stronger, as though it were fermenting. Aida aired the house, opened all the windows, and washed the sheets, pillows, and blankets. The smell only increased. Finally, she carried my grandmother's abandoned mattress all the way up to our roof to dry out in the sun.

By then, Aida's pregnant belly had started to show. It was no easy matter for her slender, awkward form to balance the heavy mattress up the spiral stairway to the roof. Looking at Aida that day, carrying the weight of her mother's cotton mattress, I could not help comparing her to my grandmother, the one solid and stubbornly fixed in the ground while my own mother seemed transient and fluid as water. I knew then that I had outgrown Aida as a mother before she had even had a chance.

Not long after, the event that I had been dreading ever since my grandmother announced it months ago to Aida over coffee came to pass—my brother Bilal was born. Contrary to what I had imagined, however, I grew extremely fond of this baby who was the picture of health and ruddy beauty and I only wished to be allowed to carry him as much as I would have liked. I felt that he smiled differently for me than for anybody else and he would even grip my hand as he lay in Aida's arms, nursing. My father and Aida, though, allotted me only moments now and then whenever they were right beside me. Their attempts to safeguard him, however, led to a secret mishap.

Going into Aida's room one morning, I found Bilal, alone, asleep on her bed. He must have been four months old at the time, with hair as black as charcoal and red cheeks. I watched him breathe, his mouth open in a tiny O, his round cheek flattened where he lay on it. I knew that he had just nursed because his open mouth was oozing milk onto the sheet. Gazing at him, listening to his short breaths, I was swept away by such a thrill of love as I had never felt before, especially with no one else in the room from whom to censor my feelings.

I tiptoed to where Bilal slept and, careful not to wake him, rolled him into my arms. Almost without realizing it, I lifted up my nightgown and placed his head at my breast, as I had seen Aida do, as I had once tried to nurse my grandmother's kittens back in Lebanon. I wanted to nurse Bilal! I nudged his cheek gently, coaxing him to open his mouth and latch onto my flat nipple. However, nursing a baby who was neither awake nor hungry was quite different from nursing eager kittens who would immediately gnaw at my skin.

Bilal was a disappointment! I was trying to return him to the bed before Aida could come back and discover us when he slipped out of my grasp.

It happened so quickly, as quickly as he must have wriggled out of Aida's belly, that I heard his head hit the tile floor before I realized what had happened. I heard his feeble wail but, too frightened to check him, I scooped him up, dumped him onto the bed, and ran out of the room.

The same guilt that infested me after my grandmother's death crept into me once more, sinking deeply into my skin like a tick.

ISABEL

7

My hair falls over one shoulder, baring one ear in the classic style of the seductress. The image pleases me; I know that Saqr will like it. I have combed my hair like this several times this week to make sure it would be just right, just as I have practiced how I will smile to indicate just the right amount of reluctance and yet willingness, memorized what I will say. All has been carefully studied and timed to heighten his desire without putting him off by my eagerness.

I look at my gold watch, the graduation gift from my father. It is past seven and Laila is still not here.

It is not unusual for Laila to be late, but neither is it her way to disregard something of this magnitude, something involving secrecy and danger. It would not be like her to miss the occasion of my plunge, my undoing, for as nonchalant as Laila pretends to be, certain things can drive her to distraction and my reticence is one of them. Besides, she has a new MG, a gift from her brother, which she is dying to show me. She will not miss tonight.

Ever since she first entered my consciousness, the day at school when she scoffed at the lunch while the rest of us dutifully ate our eggs and sandwiches and drank the last dregs of lentil soup, Laila had lain in wait for me to come alive. Like the sister I had often imagined but would never have, she was always one step ahead of me, always looking back, urging me to keep up. Perhaps it was only I who was striving to keep up with her in some hopeless way, for we were—in many ways—as different from each other as only sisters could be. I admired her, envied her, loved her, and sometimes hated her. She, in turn, was utterly bewildered by me.

Laila was worldly in other ways, too, that I knew nothing about. There was a teacher in school that I particularly liked named Miss Selwa. Like many of the teachers, she was Lebanese. She had long brown hair that she twisted and doubled into a loop, like a rope. Sometimes, toward the end of the afternoon, her hair came loose and swung down her back like a meandering serpent as she wrote in colored chalk across the blackboard. She even brought in games for us to play after our work was done—checkers, "snakes and ladders." Each of us in the second grade was a little in love with her and secretly vied to be her favorite.

Miss Selwa was engaged to be married. She boarded in the school along with the other unmarried teachers since it was forbidden for single women in Kuwait to live alone in an apartment. One night, her fiance was found, by the school guard, in the teacher's lounge long past evening visiting hours were over and he was arrested and thrown in jail. I got to know of this because my father was called in to talk to the police to help get Miss Selwa's fiance out of jail. Why the school principal thought to call my father was a mystery except that perhaps he was thought to be sympathetic, more open-minded, since his wife was an American.

For some weeks, Miss Selwa barely talked, walking about the school with her head lowered, hardly smiling any more. There were no more games in class. Then one morning we were faced with a substitute who announced that Miss Selwa was leaving the school. The other teachers looked relieved, as though Miss Selwa's pretty face was becoming a great embarrassment. Some of the older girls began to whisper about her.

While I stood at the school gate waiting for my driver, Miss Selwa carried her suitcase out to her waiting fiance. Her eyes were red and her nose and mouth were puffy, as though she had a bad cold. I ran and pressed against her. I thought that I heard her heart beating between us, but she seemed too tired and distracted to stoop to kiss me.

Years later Laila could not believe that I never knew that Miss Selwa had left school because she was pregnant.

In the school festival at the end of the second grade, our class put on a musical play about a flower garden. It reminded me of our garden back in New York, but for most of the Kuwaiti girls, then, when water was still scarce, the flowers must have seemed truly a figment of the imagination. Since I was the tallest girl in our class, with long, thin legs, I had the main role of the flower stem. I went on stage first, stood in the center in a green, crepe-paper skirt, and sang about being a leafy, green stem to an audience of somber, black-cloaked women with sparkling, gold lame masks. I spotted my mother, tall and lanky in her sleeveless summer dress, looking vulnerable with her red hair and pink skin as a freshly skinned rabbit. But this vulnerability was merely my illusion. For my mother, unlike me, was oblivious to being so different from the others.

My mother had not been the only conspicuous presence in the audience that afternoon. There was another woman with pale flesh, a woman with short brown hair that curled about her cheeks, who stared up at the stage, smiling. I turned my head enough to see that Laila had stepped into the center of the stage. Laila, in her lusty, vermilion paper skirt, sang about being the red rose. As she sang, her black lashes lowered to touch the white of her cheeks as she blushed. So, it was her mother smiling up at us. I had never seen Laila's mother before, yet I knew her at once because she was beautiful, like Laila, with scarlet lips. She was paler than pale, pliant as dough, as though a person could twist her into a thousand shapes without breaking a bone in those plump arms. She appeared to notice only Laila as she smiled up at us, revealing a brilliant, gold front tooth.

The older girls performed a traditional Kuwaiti song and dance about pearl fishing. In fluorescent dresses over which they wore translucent, sequined gowns, they rocked forward and back, side to side, to the intoxicating rhythms of drums and tambourines. They occasionally touched the tips of their noses with their fingers as they swayed, their schoolgirl braids unraveled for the occasion so that their hair fell in thick, velvet waves down their backs. Whenever they flung their heads forward, their hair would touch the floor and it was as though the stage were suddenly deluged by a swirling, black flood. So mysterious and beautiful were they as they danced, so hypnotic the spray of glitter on their dresses, that all at once I hated my light skin and hair and wished, instead, that I could somehow grow up to be one of those stunning dark girls.

It was during second grade that I began to feel invincible. Of course I knew that I was physically different from everyone else in school, even a downright oddity. I realized, too, that I was treated differently from the rest of the girls. Sometimes I thought it had to do with my mother being American, that this was thought to make me special, somehow. Later, however, I learned

42

that my father had warned the teachers that they were not to touch me—not to pull my ears or smack me with a ruler on the palms of my hands as they sometimes did to punish the other girls.

Once, in fourth grade, the entire class was punished, each girl smacked five times with a ruler, because the teacher could not find the money she had left in her drawer. The teacher, Miss Nawal, bore a deep resemblance to the film star—Gina Lollobrigida—whom I had seen on the cover of one of my mother's magazines. Miss Nawal had those same lively, sparkling eyes and buxom figure, and she was totally ruthless. On the day of the theft, the day that she punished us, she was so angry that she had deep, wet crescents under her arms.

When she reached my desk she looked at me somewhat regretfully and said, "You didn't steal, Isabel, did you?"

"No, Miss."

So, she passed on to the next girl and smacked her. Yet I wanted her to hit me because this isolation, this being singled out, was almost a worse punishment than the ruler. By treating me better than the rest, she had made me an outcast. Even Laila was slumped over her desk with her face buried in her arms. I cried along with the other girls, although for a different reason.

In order to justify the teachers' deference towards me, to rid myself of guilt, I plunged into my studies.

At the end of each quarter, in the morning after the anthem and the *fatiha*, the headmistress stood before the school and read off the names of the top three girls in every class. For many years, I was among those called to stand beside her at the head of my classmates, proud of my efforts. As usual, the competition between Laila and myself for this selection was fierce, but whereas I liked the challenge, Laila was less enthused. In an especially crude show of arrogance one term, in an effort to put me in my place, Laila nicknamed me *Abrass*—Albino.

43

LAILA

8

Starting school in Shuaiba diverted me somewhat. On the morning I was to go, Aida examined me carefully to be sure that I was neat, then she combed and braided my dark hair and tied the ends with two large, white ribbons. Sameer watched as I kissed Bilal good-by and I could feel his jealousy of the baby, although he tried to cover it. He, too, was off to school, but he ran out ahead of me since the boys' school started ten minutes before the girls' school.

I hesitated at our door, imagining for a moment that I was back in our white village in Lebanon where the voice of the sweet roll vendor in the road announced each day, and the smell of my grandmother heating *samne* to fry my egg filtered into my bedroom.

I joined the other girls on the way to school, confident of my popularity. With my grandmother gone, I had sought out the girls in the Shuaiba alleys more and more out of immense loneliness and also because of another feeling: a sudden freedom that I had never known when she was alive. Aida was more permissive and I enjoyed venturing out on my own. The Kuwaiti girls were kind, friendly and simple. Many of those on my street seemed quite poor, their houses had hardly any furniture. Their mothers rarely went out in the street but they gave me tea and cardamom cookies when I went to play in their courtyards.

The first minutes of that first day at school led me to believe that maintaining my lead among my fifteen classmates would be simple. How was I to know that my position would be challenged only too soon by a girl even more intriguing than myself?

No sooner had we been assigned seats in our new classroom that overlooked the sandy beach than a tall man and an imposing woman with hair the color of the sunrise stopped at the door of our classroom. The class fell suddenly silent. Even I, who had seen red hair in Lebanon, stared at the woman and at her strange, bleached skin. Holding onto her hand was a girl our own age who had the same hair and pallor as the woman. The two of them were astonishing, their skin like buffed ivory, their hair like crowns. It took us all several minutes to realize that the girl was being placed in our class and was being given a seat next to skinny Aisha Rashid.

I knew that I would have to establish myself all over again the moment I saw that flame of orange hair. My heart sank at that instant, not only because this startling creature—Isabel—was not seated beside me, but because I could see that she would be my nemesis.

Isabel had only to appear in the doorway of our classroom that morning to prove herself. She was unique. Anyone could see that. She was odd, too, of course, but somehow that made her even more powerful. She had an aura about her, an untouchable circle through which none of us could enter.

Once the teacher forced us to settle down and stop leaning forward to try to touch Isabel's chalky arms and blazing hair, I was able to study her from where she sat two desks ahead of me.

She was as quiet as a mouse, not looking at anyone or seeming to understand anything that was said to her. That was because she was—as the girls called her—*Englisia,* an English girl, although we were to learn later that her mother was American and her father was Arab. Only once, when a girl ran up to the blackboard during break and made faces at us, did Isabel break into laughter along with the rest.

I began to think of a way to win her.

Despite myself, I found myself wanting to be her friend. Also, having learned early on from my grandmother that people admired strength, I decided that the sooner I displayed my own strengths, the better chance I had of keeping this girl in her place.

My chance came at lunch time. We were led out of class, first to a room where we were measured for uniforms and school shoes and given books, notebooks, pencils, erasers, and white ribbons to tie in our hair. Then we went to a large hall with rows of tables and chairs and a smoky smell of cumin and lentils. I went blind from the aroma! Too excited to eat the egg that Aida had fried for me at breakfast, I had deposited it in the flower pot in our courtyard and joined the girls on their way to school on an empty stomach. Now, my insides were growling. I was famished. I could not wait to get a mouthful of food.

At first, I was too hungry to notice that Isabel stood behind me or that she sat right down next to me. I had eyes only for the slabs of white bread and cheese that were put on my plate along with a single boiled egg and a tin cup of yellow, lentil soup.

Then, suddenly, I looked about me. Everyone seemed to be eating at once, chewing and slurping greedily. I stared at the white cup with blue and orange flowers on it, watched the steam rise from the thick soup. I glanced at the pale girl beside me who was carefully biting into the bread the color of her slim fingertips.

49

That was when I decided to ignore my pleading body. I ignored my eager taste buds, too, slowly pushing my plate away. Finally, I shoved my steaming cup away and turned by back on the food.

Leaning against the table, stretching out my legs, watching as the multitude of other girls plunged their faced into their plates, I felt incredibly satisfied, more stuffed than if I had eaten twice as much as any of them. I was the most blessed girl in the world! For next to me, Isabel had completely stopped chewing and sat staring at me, her cheeks full, as though her very teeth would fall out in surprise.

Isabel and I did become friends, however.

Despite her red hair and green eyes the color of the sea just outside our school playground, I was able to hold my ground as the only Lebanese in the class. Several of our teachers were Lebanese and took a special interest in me. The Syrian and Egyptian teachers, too. Also, although the sun turned my skin brown in the long summer afternoons playing in the alleyways of Shuaiba, in winter my face grew white again, glowing with the rosiness that the other darker girls and my teachers found so curious. I was also saved from obscurity because I was prettier than Isabel. Isabel could not deny this.

Isabel's name was frequently on my tongue at home and I yearned to show Aida this girl of whom I talked so much. It was not until a few years later, however, that Isabel, who did not live in Shuaiba but rather with the other foreigners in a special compound several miles up the coast, was allowed to walk home from school with me. I had not realized how bothersome this walk would prove to be until the Shuaiba boys who went to the school next to ours and were not accustomed to Isabel's hair and eyes began to run after us, hissing at her as though she were a cat. Even Sameer, who usually lurked about in the road after school, joined his friends in the jeering.

Aida had cooked my favorite dish of green beans with tomatoes and rice that day, and I showed Isabel how to use her
fingers and the flat, round bread to soak up the sauce. Aida sat
with us on a stool in the corner of the kitchen, fascinated,
holding two-year-old Bilal who squirmed incessantly in her lap
to get a glimpse of the strange girl who dabbed inexpertly at
her food.

"Your mother's pretty," Isabel said to me, later.
"Isn't your mother?"
She considered this a moment. "Not as pretty as yours."
I had just washed our dishes and was boiling coffee for my
father and a guest who had come home from work with him.
Just then, as though to prove Isabel's point, Aida walked into
the kitchen. She had changed into a silky, new dress and had
painted her eyes with fresh, black kohl. Without a word, as
though she barely saw us, she took the tray of coffee from me
and disappeared, leaving a storm of jasmine perfume in her
wake.
Isabel and I were sent to occupy Bilal in the courtyard and
he ran from one to the other of us stumbling and squealing
with laughter at Isabel.
"When can I come to your house?" I asked Isabel, suddenly. I
was tired of playing with Bilal, tired of my house, of my family. I
wanted to see this compound where Isabel lived, to play in her
pink room that she had described to me in detail with the toys
that she had brought with her from America. But it was more
than curiosity that spurred me to invite myself to Isabel's home.
It was a certain knowledge, a terror, that I would suffocate if I
could not escape my own.
"Come tomorrow," Isabel said, without hesitation.
"I could ride home in your car," I said, satisfied.
"Let's ask your mother," she said.
I looked about me. My father stood in the shadows of the

51

sitting room, alone, smoking a cigarette. Something in his stance, the way that he seemed to hold the smoke within himself a long while before releasing it into the dark air told me that my mother was not to be disturbed. I was suddenly reminded of that day in Lebanon when I had watched him smoke a cigarette in the street outside my grandmother's house while, inside, Aida argued with her mother about us having to move to Kuwait.

Only after Isabel's driver came to fetch her home, after my friend had gone, promising to take me home with her in that same white car the following day, did I see Aida return to the sitting room. A moment later, my father's guest left.

"You idiot," Sameer said when he came home that night. "How could you bring that girl here?"

"Isabel's my friend. I'm going to her house tomorrow," I said.

"No, you're not," he said.

"She's going to take me in her car," I added, smugly, knowing that this part would make him burn with jealousy.

"You're not going—and she's not coming back here!"

"I am going!" I screamed back. "She said I could!"

Now Sameer's eyes did burn, but not with jealousy. His voice was flat, cold: "She would never invite you if she knew your mother was a whore."

His words thundered down on me. I did not understand what he meant, but I knew he had said something terrible about Aida.

I started to cry, confused and angry that he was threatening to disrupt my plans for the next day. Isabel had liked Aida. She had said that she was pretty. She had invited me to her house in the compound and I was going to go!

Sameer took a step toward me. I knew that he was sorry he had spoken so harshly. But before he could say another word, before he could explain what he meant, I made a fist and punched his stomach with all my might.

One spring morning, about a year later, my father appeared in the doorway of our classroom. I did not recognize him at first. He wore a dark suit and dark glasses and looked from one girl to another until his gaze fell on me.

A flood of memories washed over me as we walked home together in silence on that cool March day, one of the few cool days in the short desert spring. I dared not ask him why he had come for me, but I assumed that it was for the same reason that he and Aida had come to Grandmother's house that morning in Zahle several years ago—we were going to move yet again to some new place where he could finally make enough money for us to live like kings.

When we reached our alley, however, he stopped. A hush settled about us, hovered above the unpaved patch of road leading to our house. The dusty realm outside our blue, front door where I played nearly every afternoon with my friends appeared strangely alien to me now, empty at this time of day when everyone was still at school. Suddenly, yet very gently, as though afraid he might break it, my father took my hand in his. We started down the road.

All at once, I realized why the alley looked so changed. The mud walls near our house were streaked with black and at the end, where our blue door used to be, was a dark, smoking hollow. What I mistook for an instant to be the call to prayers in the still air were, instead, a woman's screams.

An instant rush of love engulfed me. Then the panic rose along my spine.

"Aida!" I cried, and started running towards the sound.

My father caught me and tried to hold me still but I wriggled free.

"Aida!"

"She's all right," he called after me, his voice breaking.

I stared at the blackened windows and walls of our house. Gray dust—ashes—blew about the courtyard, coating the white jasmine blossoms and pink oleanders still intact in their tins. The wails stopped briefly and then started again, filling the dark shell that had been our home.

My father caught up with me. He took off his dark glasses. His eyes were red and as hard as stone.

"There's been a fire—after you left for school."

I felt dizzy. "Aida?"

"Aida was out."

"Why is she screaming?" I said, suspicious, covering my ears. "Where's Sameer?"

"Sameer is with her, inside."

I found this strange. Sameer was rarely with Aida these days. Then my stomach tightened. "Bilal?"

Bilal was dead.

He had been taking a nap. By the time Aida had returned from the neighbor's house next door where she often drank morning coffee, and had run through the flames into his bedroom, it had been too late. Bilal had already suffocated.

Bilal!

At first, I screamed like Aida, howls that broke the thin air of the spring day. I screamed until I was weak, until all of Shuaiba seemed to be burning along with my house, with my baby brother. Bilal—the one sparkle of joy in my life. Without him I could not go on!

I do not remember what else happened that day but later that evening Isabel and her parents came to see us. They brought toys, blankets, and a big chocolate cake. As Isabel watched, I swallowed mouthfuls of the cake, trying to taste the sweetness, to drown in the chocolate that would take away the bitter emptiness of the terrible and inconceivable loss, that would ease my fury at Aida for having left our baby in the house alone.

Still later, after Isabel and her family left, after the neighbors had taken us to their house and spread mattresses for us to sleep on their sitting room floor, after my father had calmed Aida somewhat, Sameer came up to me.

In the dark, I felt him shudder beside me, felt his tears on my shoulder as he touched my hair every now and then to ease his own pain.

I did not move away from him as I usually did. Instead, I allowed him to soothe me, allowed his muffled croons to ease the shock of what had happened and his fingertips to stroke away Aida's sharp, fitful moans that pierced my dreams throughout that long night.

ISABEL

9

It will be unheard of, two girls driving through the desert alone at night to a seaside fortress, unchaperoned. It is something only Laila could have talked me into doing—out of sheer daring, amusement perhaps, or curiosity to see whether I will actually go through with it—and it is only something that I, so blindly wild about Saqr, would have the courage to do.

It is to the Tower of Dreams that we are going, the lone mud castle on the sea, several miles to the south of our compound. We will leave the compound and drive along the desert road that leads to the desolate sweep of oil fields.

But long before the oil fields, we will turn left at a stone marker and drive across the sand to the sea and the high walls of the Tower where Saqr has given the guard orders to admit us.

I am not sure when I first saw the Tower—its wind-worn turrets fade into my consciousness as though I had come across them over and over again before fully realizing it—I only remember when I first learned its name and felt it sealed into my memory, forever.

It was during one of my afternoon horseback rides with my father when I was, perhaps, nine. He had been riding *Noor*, Light, the frisky white mare that only a strong rider could handle, while I was on the older, gentle *Hidiya*, Gift, a small brown mare my parents had given to me on my eighth birthday.

Besides boating, riding had become a popular pastime among the expatriates in Kuwait, especially among the Texans. Stunning Arabian horses could be purchased from the Saudi bedouins in the South and there was even an informal riding club with a stable right in our compound.

My father and I always rode alone since my mother feared horses and he and I enjoyed this time together as he taught me not only to ride but to experience nature—the desert hares, the huge lizards that lumbered across the sand like prehistoric predators, the occasional scrawny fox or wild dog. Miles and miles of desolate beaches of the turquoise Gulf were ours to explore and for more of a challenge, we galloped inland, up and down the soft dunes and over the clumps of camel grass where we came upon bedouin tents, often with large American cars parked out front alongside the grazing goats. Only on Fridays, the sabbath, were there people on the beaches, picnickers fleeing the stifling city and towns with their umbrellas, blaring radios, and a lamb or chicken to roast on a spit. On those days we abandoned the beach to ride into the drab, dry wastes of the desert.

Once, we had even ridden up to the side of the road that led from Saudi Arabia up to Kuwait to watch as the Saudi King, Saud bin Abdul-Aziz, rode in his glistening black car across the 45-mile long 'neutral zone' between the Saudi and Kuwaiti borders on a state visit to the Emir of Kuwait. I had been wildly excited to see a real king and like the others who lined the road to get a glimpse of him I waved deliriously when he passed. He waved back, of course, to all of us. But in that stately, smiling face behind the smoky glass I thought he looked sad, as though he would have perhaps traded his spot in the car to be out on the road on horseback as we were, as his own father and grandfather had ridden camels.

The time that I first recall seeing the Tower, however, was on a cool November afternoon. The sand of the beach was pock-marked from an earlier, pelting rain giving it a crisp, grainy texture and, as usual, we had the stretch to ourselves—the sound of breaking waves, the gray sky, the rays of sun sifting through the still-heavy clouds as though they were God's eyes staring down at us. Across the magenta water, whitecaps nipped at the horizon. The high tide forced us to ride up where the sand was deep and it crunched under the horses' hooves like bits of ground glass.

We rode further south along the coast than usual that afternoon, passing the scattered ruins of several one-room hovels that appeared ancient but in the harsh climate might have been abandoned only a year ago. The further toward Saudi Arabia we rode, the more dramatic the topography. Monotonous flatness gradually grew into ridged elevations and lagoon-like inlets. The soft line of sandy shore gave way to undulations of hard sandstone. The sea was rougher, too, and had gouged deep grooves into the sandstone, sculpting it into endless, twisting curves.

Suddenly, ahead of us, where the ground soared to a steep ledge, stood a large, crumbling fort.

I reined in Hidiya. "What's that?"

My father halted. "It must be the Tower."

"The Tower?"

"The Tower of Dreams," he said, looking as surprised as I to

61

find the sand-colored edifice that had materialized before us.

We stared up at the lacy turrets and steep wind towers. It resembled the Medieval Arab castles in our history books, only smaller. It certainly appeared to be older than anything I had ever seen in Kuwait. Perhaps it was the 18th-century Portuguese 'little fort' that Kuwait had been named for.

"It's a castle, or a fort," I said, giddy with excitement and mesmerized by the archaic name my father had given it: 'Tower of Dreams'.

He laughed. "No, it's not a fort. It's a rich man's summer house."

I was skeptical. "It doesn't look like a summer house."

Most of the arched windows which were sunken into the forbidding, dilapidated walls seemed too high up to offer a view from within. I could not envision anyone, let alone a rich man, coming to these ramparts to escape the heat! Then, something above the structure caught my eye: Television had been introduced to Kuwait only a few months earlier and the single antenna poking up from the highest turret suddenly, oddly, linked this 'tower' to our present.

It continued to stare down at us like some lonely, clumsy apparition, at once beckoning to us and repelling us. Even the horses seemed to stall and shuffle in the sand rather than go forward.

Then, my father told me about the Tower of Dreams, how less than a hundred years ago when there was still a slave trade in Arabia, African slaves were brought across the ocean from Zanzibar and held inside the fort until they were sold to work in the households of wealthy merchants.

Horrified, I pressed my knees into Hidiya's narrow back as I envisioned the wooden, hand-sewn *jalibuts* and *Sambuqs*, like the ones used by fishermen in Shuaiba, groaning over angry seas, transporting their human cargo to this very beach. I imagined the captives wading ashore—velvet-skinned dark women like Hassa and Fatima who cleaned our school, men like gentle

Omar the school's cook, girls like Sara who was quickest at math sums and whose shrill voice and wide smile could incite us to laughter any time it pleased her. Those people had been slaves?

"Their parents and grandparents," my father said.

"And the 'dreams'? Why is it the 'Tower of Dreams'?"

My father shrugged. "It's just a fancy name."

The air about us was still as though all life had been siphoned out of it. The sky seemed heavier, as if it might unleash another rainstorm. My father grabbed Hidiya's bridle which had slipped from my fingers and pulled her behind Noor, back in the direction from which we had just come.

For a brief, uneasy moment, as we headed back up the beach, I was inside those walls breathing the heat and the dust, the sweat of the prisoners. I could smell the incense and sweet, spicy fragrance that always clung to Hassa and Fatima and even to Omar and felt I could never again look at them without feeling sad.

It seemed an abominable place, the high walls and tiny windows built to entrap and stifle the dreams of anyone who entered. Yet, strangely enough, almost in a perverse premonition, I wanted to enter that very fortress, that 'Tower', where I saw myself suffocating in some mysterious pleasure.

10

Not long after that, when I was nine, a man walked down a corridor towards me, stepping briskly, eagerly, his face beaming. My heart leapt and knew happiness as I had never known it, a thrill that was so full and smothering that it was impossible to contain. With sheer delight, I stood to run toward him, knowing that everything was suddenly wonderful—all because this man was walking down the hall toward me, because he had come to see me!

But I could not run to him. I was in a hospital that evening and the man walking toward me was my father. That this should be one of the most striking images I retained from my childhood was not surprising. My father was the single most powerful presence in my life. He was exuberant in love and in anger, rewarding much too generously and punishing severely. Yet, he seemed capable of all things, especially of a great and singular love for me. He was the provider of love, comfort, and safety. As I waited for him to reach me where I sat in a wheelchair, he resembled not so much my father as an angel from heaven.

I had been in the hospital for more than a week, recovering from a concussion. This was brought on because a week earlier, I had foolishly done something I was strictly forbidden to do—I had saddled up my father's mare, Noor, and ridden out of the stable, alone.

It had been a sunny, February afternoon. I had been bored and, having nobody to play with, I had ridden my bike the half-mile to the stables to see the horses.

Noor had been prancing about the corral when I reached it and I had watched her kick her slim legs and buck her head, then pause to listen to the air as though someone were whispering to her. I often watched Khosro, the Baluchi stable boy who was scarcely taller than I, ride Noor out of the stable for her daily run on the beach or for a bath in the sea. Unlike my tall and husky father, the wiry Khosro could perch like a bird on Noor's back, light as air, as he raced her across the sand. With her white mane flying and her tail snapping like a whip, Noor would disappear over the bluffs above the beach until only Khosro's black hair and a stream of silvery tail against the blue water were visible.

Sure enough, it was glorious on Noor's back! I, too, could be like the wind as I leaned over her neck, my legs straining to grip her broad belly. I urged her on toward the beach, all at once deciding to ride all the way to the Tower of Dreams whose sandstone walls and curling turrets had summoned me back in my imagination countless times since I had first seen them last November. I knew I had to see it again. The moment I reached the beach, in fact, I knew that this was why I had saddled up Noor. For it was on an elegant, commanding animal such as she, rather than my own small, gentle Hidiya, that one rode up to a palace!

As Noor began to canter along the water's edge where the sand was wet and hard and pocked with small crab holes, I felt

65

as sure of finding the Tower as if I had been there a thousand times before, so lucid was the image before me. But no sooner had we started along the beach, Noor already panting, a white lather foaming beneath the harness against her chest, when she stumbled. I slipped off to the side, my foot sliding all the way through the stirrup of my English saddle.

That was what I was later told, for I had no recollection of the accident, neither of hitting my head on the ground nor of being dragged, my foot caught in the saddle, a good way down the beach. It was Khosro who had relayed these events to my father, he who had spotted the frightened, galloping mare and the fluff of red hair and had run madly after us and caught Noor, then carried me home, sure that he had lost his job for not preventing me from taking the horse out of the stable.

It had taken me two weeks to come this far, to stand on my wobbling legs and try to run into my father's arms. The days after the fall were still a jumble in my mind—mainly of long conversations in Hindi being conducted by the hospital's Indian nurses as they hovered about me. These bronze-skinned 'sisters' in their blue uniforms and starched, white handkerchiefs on their heads were constantly changing my sheets, gently clicking their tongues in disapproval because I refused to eat anything, smiling when I tried to mimic their rapid, musical Hindi.

During those first few days, I could remember only snatches of visits with my father who tried to feed me food brought from home. I thought I remembered a visit paid me by Laila and her mother in which I insisted that my name was Laila and called her mother "Mama." That memory was especially soothing because Laila's mother had looked like a doll in her pastel dress and candy-pink lipstick. Of course, I heard no end of my lapse during this visit when I returned to school to find that Laila had spread the word that I had become senile! My mother was not at the hospital the day that Laila and her mother came to visit, nor on all those days that I refused to eat, or the evening that my father strode down the hall.

During the first week after the accident, I was delirious and not aware of much except the occasional face of my father and the marked absence of my mother. Perhaps that was why I insisted on not eating—I wanted my mother's food, proof that she still existed. Perhaps that was why I wanted Laila's frothy, tender mother to be my own that day they visited me although she clearly was not the tall, angular woman I knew to be my mother. Even as I sat studying that delightful concoction who continued to smile as she ordered Laila to give me a drink of water, to arrange my pillow, to get off the edge of the bed so as not to cramp my legs, I yearned for my mother's slim, freckled arms, for her familiar aroma.

It was only toward the end of my hospital stay that a sleek, copper-haired woman entered my room one morning, stepping softly across the sterile floor to sit in the vinyl chair at the window. She wore an aqua, cashmere sweater, loosely crocheted, that suddenly flooded the room with color, mirroring her blue eyes.

"Is it really you?" I said, suddenly overwhelmed.

"Yes, darling."

"Are you a ghost?"

She broke into laughter and I realized how silly this sounded, fearing at once that I would scare her away if she were, indeed, a ghost. But it *was* my mother. In a jovial voice, she told me the latest neighborhood gossip—a long-time bachelor friend had finally become engaged, Andrea Deer's mother was expecting a baby. During the entire visit, however, she never once explained her absence.

Only later did I learn that the reason she had not visited me sooner was because she had been in the hospital, herself, suffering from pneumonia. I did not remember her being sick before my fall, but the possibility that the pneumonia was a result of shock and fear for my life after my accident made me suddenly aware of her deep, though undemonstrative, love for me.

That night in the hospital, however, as my father hugged me and said that I would be coming home in a few days, once I could walk better, I could only think that he was the most important thing in my life. Perhaps out of a childish, selfish need to be the center of attention, I felt sure that in my father's affections I had no rival.

Yet, I was also aware, quite early on, that I was not alone in being bewitched by my father. Besides being undeniably hand-some, my father possessed a rare combination of energy and invincibility that proved irresistible to women. I saw it in the shy eyes of my Arab teachers whenever he came to school to talk with them about my progress—I even overheard one of them remark that it was a pity for such a man to be wasted on a foreign woman. But I also saw it in the dewy eyes of the less discreet expatriate women who seemed compelled to hover close to him whenever my mother gave a party.

As though oblivious to all of this, however, my father seemed to direct his love only toward my mother and me. It surrounded me, engulfed me, and imprisoned me. Safe within this strong-hold of love, I also yearned to escape it. Perhaps that was why when the time came to replace his fatherly adulation with the attentions of a stranger, I settled for no less than the equally imposing master of the Tower, himself—Saqr bin Ahmad.

Of course, at that time, I had not yet met Saqr. I knew only the Tower, and the power it already held over me. Yet, I was to be kept away from it for what was to seem an interminable time because after the accident I was barred from riding. What I assumed to be my father's obstinacy turned out to be my mother's resolve that I never climb onto another horse's back. Although my mother would eventually change her mind, it was over six months—the time it took my father to convince her

that I should be allowed to ride again, but only with him—
before I ever got to the Tower again.

11

Laila lived in Shuaiba, not far from our school. One day, in the third grade, I told my mother not to send the driver for me after school because Laila had invited me to go home with her.

I had never visited Laila at home but I knew where she lived because my driver had given her a lift after school on several occasions. The best part about going to visit her was that I would walk home with her and the other girls.

Laila and I left the school and headed down the empty dirt road toward the Shuaiba marketplace. The boys' school next door had just been dismissed so for a few minutes there was still a lulling, intact quiet pervading the smoldering afternoon.

I was jubilant and yet ambivalent at the freedom to walk in the streets, as though I suddenly had been let out of prison with no idea where to go or what to do. We walked with the other girls past the small shops, past the steaming, pressing shop where Indian men in *dhoties* and pajama pants stood pressing the Kuwaiti men's long, cotton *dishdashas*, women's long cotton dresses, girls' and boys' school uniforms. We passed old men squatting or sleeping in shaded alleyways. From an ornately carved wooden door left ajar came faint kitchen sounds along with the smell of hot bread and—what by now had become a familiar scent to me—rice cooking in the perfume of orange saffron.

We came to a light blue wooden door that Laila deftly kicked open. She led me down a dark corridor to a sunny courtyard surrounded by rooms. Several stools and a table stood against one wall of the patio and in each corner was a large rusting tin, the sort generally used to store olives in, here filled with blooming petunias and jasmine bushes.

Water streamed onto the patio from inside the house where swishing noises accompanied the shrill singing of a woman on a radio. All at once, a torrent of dusty water landed in a puddle at our feet.

"Mama!" Laila shouted.

A pretty woman in a cotton house dress hoisted above her knees emerged from a door and stood looking at us, broom in hand, a flowered scarf wound tightly about her head.

"So, you've brought her," the woman said, looking pleased.

"Mama, we're hungry," Laila said, flinging her satchel into a corner of the patio.

Her mother continued to stare at me, smiling, wiping her brow with the back of her plump hand.

"You must feed her," she said.

"Sit down," Laila said, pulling up a stool for me.

Minutes later, she came out of the kitchen holding two bowls of rice smothered in a stew of green beans and tomatoes. She gave me a spoon and we sat in the warm courtyard and devoured the meal, savoring the beans' greenness, the onions and cinnamon, the tomatoes as sweet and ripe as Laila's mother.

Laila had two brothers. Sameer, two years older than we, followed us home from the boys' school. Tall and brutish, he looked nothing like Laila or her mother. Bilal, the baby, had

71

the rosy skin and dark, dancing eyes of his mother. Being an only child, I was fascinated by Bilal. I stood him up and coaxed him to walk on his curved, unsteady feet. That made him squeal with laughter and soon Laila was annoyed that all I wanted to do was play with her brother.

Later that afternoon, Laila's father came home. He was short, with a heavy belly and a mustache. He brought a guest with him and Laila was sent to the kitchen to make coffee. I watched her, impressed at how she boiled the dark powder in the small pot, the froth bubbling away, then poured the coffee into tiny cups on a tray. Nobody had ever taught me to do this. At home I was not considered old enough to be of much help around the kitchen.

I was further amazed when Laila's mother appeared in the kitchen to take the tray to the men in the next room. I could not keep myself from staring at her eyes that were freshly dusted with kohl and green eye shadow, her lips that were rouged, her bosom puffing out of a low-cut, shimmering dress that whistled when she moved. Her hair, earlier hidden under the scarf, now bounced about her face in brown curls and she smelled like her pungent garden, like jasmine.

Sometime later, as Laila and I sat out in the courtyard playing cards, Laila's mother entered an inner room of the house alone with the guest. He was much taller than she. She had to bend back just to smile up at him, opening her mouth enough for her gold tooth to flicker as the man slipped something into her hand.

But I had little time to dwell on the significance of this for no sooner had Laila's mother disappeared when her father called us into the formal sitting room where he was wiring up a television he had just bought. Laila began to dance around, happily. Even Sameer was impressed and squatted down to help his father adjust the antenna. We had had a television at home for nearly a year but Laila had been telling me for the

72

last six months that she was getting one. We sat on the floor watching Laila's father alter knobs and screws and hearing the sounds of an Egyptian broadcaster relay the events of a noisy soccer game before the black-and-white picture finally emerged. There was still only one channel in Kuwait at the time, and we watched the soccer game, the fifteen minutes of American cartoons which were broadcasted each evening, an Arabic show, right until the closing of the station at ten o'clock with a reading of the Qur'an. It was the first time I had sat in the same room for any length of time with Laila's father and Sameer. Her father brought us small bowls of peanuts and salted watermelon seeds as we stretched out on the floor.

Later, Laila's mother joined us. She, too, seemed mesmerized by this new acquisition and made us tea and brought us slices of cold melon to nibble on. Her engaging smile and soft, shapely body seemed particularly fragile that night, although she laughed and clapped along with us at the various programs we watched. By now I was convinced that she was the most beautiful woman I had ever seen. I thought Laila to be very lucky. For when she grew up, she would undoubtedly be as beautiful and bewitching as her mother.

It was not until several years later, when I overheard people remarking how beautiful my own mother was—how elegant her willowy figure and how stunning her penetrating, blue eyes—that I took a second, deeper look at her. Yet, it was only later, after I met dark, impetuous Saqr, that I felt for the first time to be almost as lucky as Laila.

At the end of fifth grade, two things happened that awakened us Shuaiba girls to the reality that we did not quite believe in yet. First, I overheard my father telling my mother that there had been a terrible accident—Laila's house had caught fire and the baby was dead. After my initial numbness I started to cry, then to scream: *Bilal!*

My mother tried to calm me by telling me to help her gather blankets and food for the family.

By the time we arrived at Laila's house the fire had been put out, but the walls were streaked with black as though someone had attacked them with a piece of charcoal. I could hear Laila's mother's periodic screams from another room, a terrible howling.

Laila, herself, seemed to be more interested in the chocolate cake my mother brought than anything else, stuffing chunks of it into her mouth and then vomiting it up as she suddenly remembered what had happened. I stood numbed, trying to keep out of the way of the men carrying things in and out as though the family were simply moving, pretending not to hear the distressed, muffled voices of Laila's mother and father in the next room. Laila did not go to school for almost a week during which I had nightmares of riding Hidiya into the desert and coming across the stiff, charred remains of Bilal in the sand. I could not forget Bilal's chubby face nor his squat legs as soft as fresh dough, his ringing laughter.

The next time I saw Laila's mother was at the end of term during our yearly school play. She sat among the other black-cloaked mothers, herself in a black dress of mourning, her drawn face wan without her usual make-up. Yet while the other mothers gasped and laughed at our rehearsed antics, their eyes brightened by their daughters' reciting and dancing, Laila's mother sat through the play as if by force, barely noticing Laila's exceptional theatrics, not once smiling her pretty, glinting smile.

Then, on the last day of school, we had the second shock to take with us through the summer. Aisha Rashid, a girl who had come to surpass both Laila and myself in our studies and had thus usurped the coveted position of first place in the fifth grade, left school to be married.

It was rumored that the groom was old and already had

another wife and this absorbed the teachers and especially the older girls who felt themselves suddenly vulnerable to the unpredictable whims of their families. This news clouded the usual euphoria of year-end report cards and early dismissal, while the absence of the studious, gentle Aisha was like a placard placed in our midst to confirm this awful truth.

Aisha Rashid's father was a wiry pearl diver and, except for her long, silken braids Aisha could pass for a boy, herself, with her lean body and plain face, the brown-speckled teeth. Although physically uninspiring, however, Aisha was like the mother of us all in the fifth grade, her eyes gentle, her kindness reflecting a wisdom of the ages. It was unthinkable that her father would give her away in marriage to an old man when she was smarter and better than any of us. I was horrified whenever I pictured her toiling under the burden of several children and a husband, suddenly realizing how wasted all her hard school work had been and how selfish I was to compete with her.

Yet Aisha Rashid's marriage was only the beginning. As though drawn by some mysterious call, girls faded from our midst one by one over the next two years to get married or to help their mothers with work at home. By the seventh grade, our original thirty were down to ten.

For a long time afterwards, the memory of Bilal's death and Aisha Rashid's leaving school were intertwined, as though they were the same thing—marriage and death.

12

I was fourteen when I first met Saqr... Hawk. His eyes did not belie his name; they were narrow and slanted, shrewd. Yet they were beautiful in the context of his face which was fuller than most of the faces of the Kuwaiti men I knew, a physical type known as *Najdi,* or having come from central Saudi Arabia. He was dark, with thick, straight hair and he was tall, as solid as a dinosaur when he walked, commanding attention.

We met at the house of a Kuwaiti friend of my father's who had invited us to lunch on the first day of the *Eid al Adha* feast after the Hajj. The *Eid* had come as a surprise that day, the start of the feast always being determined by the appearance of the new moon, often late at night. I usually never knew the night before whether it was to be a holiday the next day or not until I awoke early in the morning and discovered that my father had left home at dawn to pay the customary respects to the Sheikhs after the dawn Eid prayers.

I had not wanted to get all dressed up to go to the lunch,

wanting to spend the warm March day on the beach, instead, but my parents had insisted. Saqr was there with his own father, a surprisingly ugly man whose face seemed to embody all of Saqr's features in an expanded, almost grotesque way. The men sat alone in a separate sitting room and rose to leave just as my family and I entered.

I noted Saqr briefly in those few moments, the breadth of his shoulders, his strong back, as he stood in a gold-trimmed, hazel *abaya* over a cream-colored *dishdasha*. I sensed that he had looked at me a second longer than necessary, too, although his eyes barely grazed mine when he nodded greetings and left the room behind his father, casually draping the edge of his outer *abaya* over one arm. He looked like someone's dream of a desert Arab, embodying all the eloquence of his race in that one nod and lifting of his *abaya* as if it were some royal cloak.

I was so absorbed, that I immediately forgot his name along with my earlier bad mood and the fact that I had resisted coming to the Eid lunch in the first place. I felt sure that he had taken special note of me but then wondered whether it had been more of a curiosity about my paleness or my freckles, or my hair that was streaked with blond by years in the unrelenting sun. I was not accustomed to being thought of as attractive by Kuwaitis and did not expect to draw anything other than awe from men. My impression of how men regarded me was still colored by those gleeful, boyish shouts outside our school gate: "*Quitta!* Cat! Meow!" When he left, sliding along with his father into the back seat of a large, awaiting car, I felt a deep sadness, almost a blow, as I realized that I would never be pretty enough in the conventional Arab way to attract such a man as that!

A month later I saw him again.

This time it was at a party given by Andrea Deer, my British neighbor and former school mate who lived several houses away. There was dancing to loud Beatles music when I got there. At once I felt distinctly out of place as the only 'resident'

77

since all the other guests—American and British former class-mates of mine—had long since left the compound expatriate school for boarding schools in Britain, Switzerland, or Beirut.

Home for Easter vacation, the British boys all sported Beatles haircuts and wore gray or navy blazers while the British girls were dressed in minute miniskirts. Their British accents were razor-sharp once again as they talked of the 'smashing' young Prince Charles and his sister, Princess Anne.

The Americans were more casual and even, I thought, a bit sloppy. A few of the girls with whom I used to play only a few years ago were actually lounging on the knees of various boys as though this were perfectly natural. Their talk was mostly of tennis lessons and the 'wonderful' schools they boarded at in Switzerland or Beirut; they rolled their eyes and smiled as they talked of the fun they had left behind and could not wait to get back to. I overheard several of the American boys talk in hushed, excited tones about how 'fast' the British girls were.

"So, Isabel, are you still in the local school?"

It was Andrea, her blond hair as wispy as when we were children, Andrea who had helped me bury my dead pet rabbit when we were both eight, who had poured orange juice all over my school books so that they were sticky when I arrived mid-day from Shuaiba.

Her cheeks had regained their English flush after a winter in London and she was plumper than before, not just adolescent fat but the inherited genetic roundness of her mother that was both attractive and middle-aged looking.

"Hello, Andrea," I said, hoping to rekindle our old friend-ship, "Yes, I'm still here."

"Still in Shuaiba?"

"They've just opened a new high school in Fahaheel."

Andrea smiled, flicking her blond mane. "You'd have a smash-ing time in London. You should convince your parents to send you. The boys are dreamy."

Just then, a husky American boy with a thick, marine hair-cut like a brush turned upside down came up to us. His parents had just moved to Kuwait and this was his first trip over. He attended a military school in the United States, he told us. He was a wrestler. He was attempting to be pleasant, I assumed, because aside from Andrea he seemed not to know anyone else there. In a moment, Andrea was gone and I was standing alone beside him, sipping a Coca Cola and wondering what to say to him.

Later, after he walked away, Andrea returned and told me that she had met the wrestler only the week before at a strange party they had been at. A group similar to tonight's, teenagers home on vacation, was invited to the seaside palace of a rich, local boy. It was all peculiar, magical, Andrea told me, the inside of the place was plush and all done up in red and gold. They were even served beer, usually not allowed in local homes.

The only problem was that the wrestler fellow had had a few too many beers and wandered off on his own into what turned out to be the host's father's harem.

"Sheer bedlam," Andrea snorted in laughter. "I never saw so many angry ladies in my life!"

"A harem?" I said, amused at this antiquated expression.

The host's mother, she explained, along with his aunts, sisters, cousins, and unveiled servants, had just settled down for an evening of television when the fellow ambled in on them. Horrified at being seen unveiled by a strange man, the women had scattered like chickens, the younger women had been especially embarrassed since some of them were wearing miniskirts in the privacy of their quarters. The servants immediately began shouting and waving brooms at the young man. After that, they had to break up the party and leave.

Andrea grabbed my arm. "That's *him*, the host, there!"

Three men in *dishdashas* had just walked through the front door. I recognized the tallest one: the young man I had seen the day of the *Eid*. Andrea stared at them, seemingly as transfixed as I was.

"Who is he?" I said, having forgotten his name and hoping to drown out the pounding that was rushing to my head.

"I don't know."

The other two men, I learned later, were more than his friends, they were also his personal retainers without whom he rarely went anywhere. Saqr was strange that way, but then, again, not. The desert bred a distrust of solitude and it was an innate trait of his, as well as other Kuwaitis it seemed, to be with others, to thrive on companionship. He was rarely without a cousin or a friend—except for later, when he was with me. Yet, even then I did not fill the void that only his male friends did; I simply made him forget about them, he said, forget about the brutal loneliness of living for a while.

This was it. The first tidbits of information I ever heard about Saqr were of palaces and *hareem.* What could be more fascinating yet more removed from my existence than that? He and his family were not people I would ever have known growing up as I did. Each day I shuttled between a modern twentieth-century oil camp and the medieval village of Shuaiba, trying to maintain some degree of equilibrium as I muddled through the rigors of two school curriculums, two languages, two opposing cultures with their respective sets of demands. However, I never, in all the years I lived there, came remotely close to witnessing for myself the sort of life I heard being talked about now—pleasure seekers, palaces. I did not quite believe it existed, even as I listened to Andrea, even as I saw Saqr across the room. For an instant, we seemed to have been transported out of the eternal present into some incredible and unfamiliar place.

The closest I had ever come to being inside a palace was one morning long ago when I had accompanied my father as he was inspecting a new palace being constructed for a certain Sheikh of the ruling family. As an engineer, my father was often asked to render an objective evaluation of a structure for a friend or acquaintance. What came to mind as I watched Saqr move about the roomful of foreigners, acknowledging them, nodding, smiling slightly as though he knew that he were somehow above all of them, was coming across a tiny, distant point in the desert which slowly grew as we approached it to become a colossal, rose-pink miracle in the sand. There were glossy, circular steps throughout, marble halls, and airy balconies with intricate trellises. The most delightful part of the building, it had seemed to me, were the servants' quarters—tens of tiny bedrooms, each one with a pink, tulip-like light fixture dangling from the ceiling.

"I've seen you before."

I spun around at the sudden presence behind me. He was looking at me as though undecided whether or not to smile. "The day of the Feast," he reminded me.

"Yes," I said, quickly, "I think I remember you."

"I think I remember you," he repeated, grinning, as though mocking my attempt to be detached.

He glanced about as if trying to remember where he was, how he had gotten here. His friends were waiting for him by the door as though alerted to some secret signal from him. They had not attempted to mingle with the crowd. They looked restless, like skittish colts.

I was suddenly embarrassed, aware that Andrea and some others were staring at me, no doubt wondering how I knew this man in the expensive gold-trimmed *abaya* and headdress, perhaps envying me my ability to speak to him in the Arabic they did not understand nor had ever attempted to learn. How remote I must have seemed to them as I stood talking, staring into the lush, black eyes of this 'local boy'.

Then, I, too, began to wonder what I was doing at this party and what was supposed to happen next. It seemed that this curious young man had come just for me, just to fetch me away from the Beatles and the stories of boarding schools and to

81

take me back, instead, to the sea slapping against the walls of our school, to the sand and the tents outside our compound, to girls with spicy, black hair that smelled of sweet coconut oil, girls who walked hand in hand, chanting out lessons in the mornings before classes.

Soon, we were talking as though it were perfectly natural that I spoke his desert Arabic, that I understood when he talked of horses, of falcon hunting, of sports cars and speed boats. He told me that his name was Saqr, that he had a place on the beach not far from my compound where he went on weekends. I thought of the Tower. Surely, it could not be his...

He talked again of falcon hunting with his father and he laughed—as though I had said the funniest thing in the world—when I told him that it was a pity, that it was really cheating, to hunt in jeeps with rifles the few rabbits and gazelles left in the desert. He changed the subject and told me of his father's palaces, of his father's concubines, as though he were talking to one of his male friends. He said, almost sadly, that money could buy anything, that he could have an English girl just like that if he wanted—he snapped his fingers—in exchange for his gold lighter. He said all this as though he expected me to understand perfectly.

And, somehow, I did understand. Perfectly.

When a slow song began to play on the record player and several of the boys and girls moved to the center of the room and clasped each other as they began to sway, Saqr asked me if I would like to dance. Without answering, trying to ignore the subtle smiles of his friends who still stood alone to one side of the room, I let him lead me toward the other dancers, feeling as I drew near him, as he brought his arm across my back and lowered his head gently toward my shoulder, that I was suddenly being embraced by the desert, enfolded into endless reams of sand, rocked by the gentle pulsing of the sea. I was drawn, however, to more than his rugged face, the warmth of his body, the trace of a spicy, sweet cologne like that worn by the Shuaiba girls; Saqr bore down on me like the summer sun, both unbearable and familiar, offering me a key to enter his desert world.

I was not allowed to stay past eleven o'clock and had to leave the party just as dinner was served. As my father walked me home, I realized for the first time just how sheltered I had been. I still could not believe that this young man had told me all of this with such ease. It was still the beginning, however, and I felt the jubilation of having had a conversation that would never be of any significance except for the pleasure it brought. It was the easy ecstasy that comes with falling in love before you realize it, before the passion breaks through and shatters the serenity of those first giddy moments.

"You actually spoke with him about his father's *hareem!*"

"*He* brought it up," I said.

Laila's eyes grew wide and round as moons, her eyebrows twisting in disbelief. "This *Hubara* fellow..."

"Saqr," I corrected her. Saqr was the falcon, Hubara was the bustard. The falcon hunted the bustard. I did not think Laila's joke funny.

"Anyway, who is he?"

"I don't know."

"You talked to him all evening and don't know who he is?"

I paused a moment. "I know that his name is Saqr, that his father is rich and lives in a palace with many concubines. I don't know anything else, so I don't know who he is."

"What's his name?"

"Saqr."

"Saqr *what?*" Laila sighed.

"I don't know."

"You didn't ask?"

"No."

"When are you going to pay more attention to things? You can't just talk with someone you know nothing about. Not even his name!" Laila must have seen that she was getting nowhere with me. Still mesmerized by my memories of last night, by my ability to attract this young man, I was suddenly engulfed by an unexpected happiness.

"Is he good looking?" Laila asked, finally.

"In a way."

"In what way?"

"He's like a dinosaur," I said, simply.

"A dinosaur?"

"I mean, he's big and tall..."

"Yes?"

"He's dark and his face is rather like a hawk's."

"He doesn't sound as special as all that."

I blushed, then hated myself for it.

"You really are in love!" Laila crowed triumphantly.

"I'm not!"

"Yes, you are. I can tell."

"I shouldn't have told you anything."

"Isabel is in love," Laila sang softly, mocking. Then she turned serious. "I suppose I'll have to find out who he is for you."

13

Laila took it upon herself to find out who Saqr was and with fourteen-year old dexterity, she did just that. Then, she proceeded to deliver her findings to me.

His full name was Saqr 'Abbas bin Ahmad. The bin Ahmad family, everyone knew, had been a prestigious clan of merchants long before the discovery of oil. For years, even generations, they had owned most of the ships that supplied Kuwait's drinking water which had to be brought from the Shatt-al-Arab in Iraq to then be sold to the public. They had also owned half of the pearl fleet which had been a great source of Kuwaiti wealth until the onslaught on the natural pearl industry by Japan's cheaper, cultured pearls. But, the bin Ahmad's were still powerful. Despite the government's new desalination water plants which made drinking water plentiful, and the decline in the demand for natural pearls, the bin Ahmad name was still plastered across boat yards, jewelry stores, and car dealerships in town. They even had a few family members in government, a rare opportunity if one was not a member of the Sheikhdom's royal family.

In the past, merchants of the Arabian Gulf towns had depended on business dealings with larger, thriving Iran across the Gulf, prompting Arabs traders to travel frequently to the Persian coastal cities of Hormuz, Abadan, and Khark. The bin Ahmad men had, like others, acquired a few Persian brides along the way, milk-white skinned girls like flowering carpets who imbued the Arab stock with their delicate, Parsi features. The bin Ahmad's mixed Arab/Persian lineage was not overlooked.

"*Ajam*," Laila said, emphatically, barely able to control her mirth. *Ajam* meant Persian, rather than pure Arab, a diminutive in the eyes of Kuwaitis. Saqr's grandmother, she told me, was a pure *Ajamia* from Isfahan. "But now they're marrying only Arabs again, of course, to regain their power."

By now, even Shuaiba had telephones and Laila relayed all this to me in whispers over the wire.

Saqr was, apparently, the only son although he had three sisters, Shehrazade, Fatima, and Yasamin.

"Since he's their only boy, they'll never let him love a foreign girl," Laila said, clicking her tongue. "They'll cement him to one of his cousins before he's twenty."

I hated her for saying that, for already predicting my loss, although I knew it was true. Cousins were always coveted marriage partners among traditional Arabs. My own grandparents were first cousins as was one of my uncles and his wife. It was deemed especially desirable to marry a cousin when one was from a rich and powerful family. Saqr, being attractive, wealthy, and an only son would not be wasted on a stranger. I remembered how the teachers in the Shuaiba school had commented on my own father being 'wasted' on a foreign woman.

Yet, there was also a note of approval in Laila's voice as she relayed Saqr's family tree, an expression of admiration that she could not hide, as though we had conspired together, somehow, for me to attract such a young man. She almost seemed pleased with me. Although I did not allow myself to believe for a minute that I had any claim on Saqr, I resented Laila's trying to maneuver into my life, assuming herself to be my mentor. Worse, I detected a note of envy in those incredible, bold eyes. And if this were so, if Saqr had piqued Laila's interest, then might she not become a rival to contend with?

Ajam. The word lingered in my mind exactly as Laila had pronounced it, the soft *j*, with a slightly triumphant edge. It conjured up a colorful, cool, magical world of Iran across the sea that had been linked with the Arabian coast since the beginning of time and yet was remote enough to be a fairy tale. It was a world of carpets, of artisans of brass and feather-fine paintings on ivory, a world of mountains thick with exotic fruit trees. The expatriates in our compound were always flying off to Teheran or Isfahan for short vacations to shop for carpets or to explore the exquisite, mosaic palaces and turquoise-domed mosques.

My mother had taken me to Teheran once, when I was ten, and we had been driven far out of the congested city up to the snow-capped mountains, cherry orchards, and lakes where villagers scrubbed carpets by hand, drenching them in a pool and beating them clean on the rocks. The air had been crisp and dry, the sky a royal blue, no hint of the harsh glare of sand that we had grown accustomed to in the desert.

It had felt like we were driving through heaven — plains of green pastures filled with goats and tribal women in long, vibrant dresses. We were passing through Baluchistan. When we stopped at a souvenir shop, I chose a handmade straw doll wearing layers of embroidered skirts and scarves—a Baluchi princess.

These memories were suddenly conjured up in Laila's single word, *ajam*—the clean smell of the mountains, the miles and miles of emerald surrounding the villages, the jewel-like domes and minarets of the mosques.

However, there was another memory, a different one from this childhood vacation. It had been in the middle of a winter night when I awoke to a sharp rap at my bedroom window. I had realized at once that it had been going on for some time, the sounds intruding into my dreams.

Too frightened to lift my curtain to see who it was, I had run into the living room to see if anyone else was awake. Through a moonlit window, I saw shadows darting around the outside of the house. There had been a faint noise of scrambling, like an animal pawing the walls to get in, then all was quiet again. My father was suddenly standing beside me with his flashlight. He went straight outside to the patio and I followed him.

In the distance, the moonlight was a glittering path across the calm sea. Shivering, I stood watching the several silhouettes loping along the beach. There had been a sudden crack of gunfire, then loud shouts. My father had told me to go back into the house. He had stood a moment longer before joining me, telling me that the police had taken care of it.

It was an episode we had witnessed before: men landing at our compound beach after several days' sail from Iran. Men in small boats, exhausted and half starved, risking their lives in a desperate desire to find work in this oil-soaked country to support impoverished families at home. Rarely were any of these illegal workers actually shot. Most often they were simply frightened by the Kuwaiti police into giving themselves up as it had seemed to be the case that night. *Ajam.* In the eyes of many Arabs these poorer neighbors across the sea were a nuisance.

Laila had amassed her information on Saqr and his family through a convenient medium—her brother, Sameer. She had told him what she wanted to know and Sameer had made inquiries. He was already seventeen and being a boy and free to do as he liked, he was able to ask questions without raising curiosity. He even alluded to having attended one of Saqr's alleged parties, himself.

"Where?" Laila wanted to know.

"Some remote place on the beach," he had told her. "A sort of palace made of mud."

"What about the inside?"

The inside had been opulent, he admitted. "Crystal chandeliers, velvet and gold chairs."

"Was it South? Toward the oil fields?" Laila asked.

"Yes. We drove along that road."

"What about the young man, the host?"

Sameer had shrugged. "A ladies' man, but who wouldn't be with a father that rich who had several concubines besides his wives?"

It was hard to picture Sameer recounting all of this to Laila. I had hardly heard him speak more than a single sentence at a sitting. It was even harder to imagine his taking the time to find out the details Laila wanted instead of scolding her for being interested in a young man she did not even know.

When we were younger, Sameer was bullying and a little frightening. He hardly ever spoke to me whenever I visited Laila, but his presence was forever felt, as though we could expect him, at any moment, to come out and stare at us or order Laila to go and get him something and then to scold her for not responding quickly enough. Once, in his anger at her for something trivial, he had spit at us, his saliva spraying us like bullets. Another time, he had thrown a watermelon at us.

However, these days he was civil to us, even polite. He had also grown somewhat handsome, with hazel eyes and brown hair that—like mine—had been bleached by the relentless sun. Although I had known him all those years, Sameer was still a complete stranger to me, impenetrable, blank as opaque paper upon which nothing had yet been written. Yet, Laila seemed curiously affectionate toward him, rising up to defend him whenever anyone remarked that he was such a loner.

89

15

At the end of the ninth grade, we had completed middle school and had to take state examinations to enter high school. There was also, of course, another exam to graduate from high school. Both tests were held for everyone in a central location in Kuwait city, on a specific day.

There were fifteen of us girls from the Shuaiba school going on to the new high school that had just opened in Fahaheel. There were Kuwaitis, two Egyptians, two Palestinians, then Laila and myself. We were transported by bus for an hour along a tar road that drifted like an endless spool of black thread across the sand toward the city.

The sun burned down on the tar, sending waves of heat across the road before us as though the bus were sailing across water. It was easy to half close my eyes and imagine that the bus was traversing the sea, the end of which was the distant horizon where the waves really did look blue. All around us the desert was like the ocean floor—pure, yellow, enveloping infinity.

We were quiet in the hot, unair-conditioned bus. Some girls were reviewing their textbooks. Laila dozed against the half-opened glass window as the wind blew against her face. I stared out at the scattered villas that began to appear, signaling the beginning of the city limits.

The habitual desert drabness and centuries of black, goat-hair tents and mud villages had inspired the now-wealthy Kuwaities to build the brightest, most iridescent houses possible. Unlike the pale pastels of the prefabricated houses of our compound—colors that were intended, no doubt, to blend into the surroundings—the new Arab houses of the city shouted out in their unabashed desire to be noticed.

Like our pink and blue school, these colorful, multi-floored structures were intended to inspire in their own vivid, distinct fashion. A green wall here, a yellow there, a pink veranda, a blue door were all wrapped into one confectionery delight. There were flat roofs and sloping roofs, a speckled tile facade on one side of a house, surrealist dots and squares on another. Like siblings in a large family, each one demanded attention, each trying to outdo the other. Ever since I could remember, I had wanted to live in one of those delicious houses.

Midway through the four-hour exam which we took in the dining hall of the new university under a dozen whirring ceiling fans, we were given a rest. Girls and boys who had been sitting in separate areas of the large room during the test now filed out to the sandy grounds, shyly avoiding each other as they bought cool drinks from a refreshment stand and went to sit on wooden benches that had been placed in the shade of some newly planted trees.

Laila went off to buy us a drink while I went to claim a bench under one of the fledgling, drooping oleanders. A throbbing headache that had started on the bus ride into the city had now spread across my scalp, making me slightly nauseous. I dropped

91

my head to my knees, pressing at the pain at my eyebrows with my fingertips, and thought about the disturbing rumors I had heard recently: that the chemical fumes from the refinery were becoming a health catastrophe. More and more people, expatriates as well as the Kuwaiti girls at school, were talking about the growing cases of cancer in Kuwait. The oil refineries were the supposed culprits. I had lived in Kuwait over eight years. Tired and thirsty, I now thought I could detect the fumes from our compound's ever-burning flare all the way into the city. I wondered if the refinery smoke I had been inhaling all this time had finally invaded my brain and planted a cancer on this examination day.

Then, came the voice. "It's Isabel?"

I looked up. The sun of the city seemed to shoot down sharper than it ever did in Shuaiba. I sat staring at the figure standing before me for a long, bewildered moment.

"Saqr?"

"What are you doing here? Are you graduating?" he said.

I stared up at him through a mass of pumping nerves, thinking that he might just be a hallucination, a vision brought on by my having missed him so. Then, embarrassed by my own silence, I quickly said, "No, of course not. I'm just entering high school."

"Ah," he said, smiling as he had done the last time we met, as though I had just said the funniest thing in the world. "Why, you're just a child."

Still looking up at him, I granted him a slight smile, acknowledging that I was, indeed, a child.

It was the first time I had seen him without his *dishdasha* and headdress. In the gray school uniform he looked quite human, ordinary in fact. Then, I noticed something under his jacket, something shiny and silvery that shimmered when he moved and which brought back a spark of the magic that he had

92

radiated the first time we met. It was a brocade vest with threads of black and silver spun into the silken gray fabric. Although it was a bit gaudy, even somewhat feminine, I found it fascinating.

"How did you do?" I asked him, forcing my eyes away from the vest to the hall behind him.

"I'll do better on the literature."

"I'm better at science and math. I always have been," I said, remembering my years of competing with Laila and Aisha Rashid for first place in math.

"You're too pretty to be a scientist," he said.

I stared at him, trying not to appreciate the flattery, but suddenly weak, hoping that he meant this. Then, I stood up. Laila was approaching with our drinks.

"Even your strange hair is beautiful," he said.

"Shhh!"

"I've been asking about you. I know who you are," he continued in a whisper, just as Laila reached us.

"This is Saqr," I said to her, trying to drown my stammer, quickly taking a sip from the icy, pineapple drink she handed me.

Laila and Saqr looked at one another, Laila unabashedly curious.

"Saqr bin Ahmad," Saqr said.

Laila nodded, pretending she did not already know this, then dropped her eyes. "They're going back in. You'd better come, Isabel," she said, starting off.

"Ill be right there," I called after her.

"I want to see you," Saqr said, the moment Laila was out of range. "I know that you live in the compound near Shuaiba. I know that your mother is American. I also know that you've been asking about me."

"I have not," I said, feeling my face go numb under my sweat.

"Somebody told me that a girl with red hair has been asking about me."

"They're lying. I've never asked anyone about you," I said, angry.

He was laughing now, so lightly I could barely hear. He tugged at his chin, as though he had a beard, his eyes shining.

"I have a place not far from you. It's right on the sea. I could come and take you there."

"I've got to go now," I said, shocked by his sudden, daring familiarity.

"No one ever told you that you're beautiful?" he said. He took hold of my arm. I stared at his hand which was large and well formed, at his impeccable nails. Surely, he had never had to stand at attention while his teachers inspected his nails or checked his hair for lice. A bin Ahmad would have been exempt.

I pushed his hand away.

"I can come and get you," he said, smiling again.

"I'll never come."

He looked surprised. "Why not?"

"Why should I?"

"Because I want you to."

"You're insane," I said.

"I'm insane for you," he said.

I tried to think of something to say in response when I noticed that only a few students were left scanning their textbooks in the shade of the wall.

"I'll come for you," Saqr repeated, following me as I hurried toward the building.

"No. I'll get in trouble."

"With who?"

"With my father," I said irritably, impatient with his pretense at ignorance of what girls were and were not permitted to do.

"Then, don't tell your father," he said. "Come yourself. My place is just south of your compound. It's not visible from the road until you get to the sea. If you get lost, just ask anyone how to get to the Tower."

It was all I could do to concentrate on the exam after that, aware that in the boys' section across the room, Saqr was also filling out his notebook, and knowing that this meant that he would be graduating and going away next year.

In a few weeks it was summer vacation and I did not see Saqr. He had gone off somewhere, Laila learned from Sameer, somewhere in Europe where there were cool mountains and beautiful lakes and casinos for gambling. I thought of Saqr all summer as I swam in the tepid, crystalline Gulf, or when I rode Noor—by then my small, brown Hidiya had died—and I pictured him in the intriguing silver vest, flying off on an airplane, brandishing his smile at the stewardesses.

Then, as the summer waned and Saqr's presence grew dimmer, I began to have other thoughts. I wondered whether my yearning for Saqr, to be a part of him, to be his girl, was really a yearning to be a true part of this desert which I loved so much and yet felt a stranger in, the need to stop being an outsider, an 'albino'.

16

Our first year in high school brought a certain apprehension at having to grow up. Now that we were on our way to the finish line, to graduating, we became acutely aware of ourselves as young women. Not being threatened by an early marriage and confinement in the home like some of our friends, Laila and I, none-the-less, became restless.

Gone was our familiar Shuaiba school with robust Omar to ladle out our soup, with Mariam and Hassa who had known us from first grade through puberty and who could still be counted on to spread out their arms to us, the wide sleeves of their gowns like gauzy wings, and listen sympathetically if one of us had failed a test or received some other humiliation. In the new girls' high school, ten of us from Shuaiba joined girls from three other village schools to become some forty strong in the tenth grade. Yet, although at first we felt lost, cast out of Shuaiba's snug womb into the larger world, among so many strangers we suddenly discovered a new freedom.

I was happy, in one sense, to no longer be the only redhead. An Egyptian girl with deep, auburn hair joined our ranks, although her skin was wheat-colored rather than freckled and her eyes were almost as black as Laila's. On the other hand, I was once more regarded as a foreigner in these new surroundings and most of the new girls and teachers were skeptical, or amused, at first, when I spoke to them in Arabic.

The new high school was in Fahaheel, a town built around another oil refinery but better known to us as the marketplace where we did our weekly grocery shopping. A row of food stalls had recently been covered, tiled, and air-conditioned, although it still smelled pungently of fruit, spices, fish, and freshly-butchered meat. Black-*abayaed* women in slippers and men in *dishdashas* as well as an assortment of Europeans and Americans, all lugged heavy plastic baskets full of groceries as they went from stall to stall.

There was also an outdoor row of modern shops run by Indians and Pakistanis. Besides everyday necessities such as clothing, shoes, make-up, and housewares, these stores were filled with assorted collectibles from around the globe: Indian gold-spun saris, Chinese embroidered slippers and tablecloths, ivory-inlaid tables from Kashmir, African wood carvings of nude women and long-faced men, endless racks of records of Western music. Further down the road, in an alley set off by itself, was the traditional gold *souk*, its windows crammed with glittering twenty-two carat chains, bracelets, earrings.

Since the girls in the high school came from Fahaheel, Shuaiba, and two other villages, the school had a fleet of six buses. Laila now rode a bus to and from school every day and it was she who first drew my attention to a particular bus driver.

"Why is it that I have to end up with an old man for a driver when I could have had *him?*" she asked, indignant, one afternoon at the school gate just as my own car and driver pulled up.

I followed her glance to the young man in blue jeans and a red T-shirt that clung to his back with sweat. He was slim and muscular, handsome, with a mustache growing down the sides of his mouth. We watched as he crouched to fix something on the bus's front tire, how the muscles in his arms flexed as he worked, hardening and quivering with effort. Then, all at once he stood, frowned, and kicked the tire with his foot. Laila giggled sharply, and the man turned to us, his eyes burning.

"He wants to see me," Laila said the next day in class during the history lesson.

"Who?"

"The bus driver."

"How do you know?"

"I saw him looking at me this morning when he was parking the bus. He has *eyes*."

I copied a few notes from the blackboard because the teacher was looking at us.

"He's married," Laila whispered.

I looked at her.

"He has a baby, too," she added, jabbing me in the ribs. A child, to us, was sure proof of virility.

The teacher raised her voice in a stern falsetto. "Laila and Isabel, move apart."

Laila stared at the teacher a moment longer than necessary before she gathered up her books, bending toward me as she did so to reveal a folded piece of paper stuck between her breasts at her unbuttoned uniform collar.

"Take it and wait for me after school," she said. Then, she trudged to the back of the room and flopped down noisily at an empty desk.

When the teacher resumed charting the course of the Islamic conquests under Tariq bin Ziyad, I unfolded Laila's note. Scribbled hastily were three words: "Thursday at seven."

Later, as we came out of the school gate, the young bus driver was leaning against the bus, arms folded, as though waiting for us. That time, instead of scowling, he looked Laila in the eye and winked.

"That means he wants to see me," Laila said.

"What do you mean?"

"Did you read the note?"

"You wrote, 'Thursday at seven.'"

"*He* wrote it. A girl from his bus passed it to me. He wants to meet me here before school on Thursday. That's when the drivers come to get the buses."

"And you're going to meet him? Here?"

"Of course."

"But how? Why?" I was alarmed by her sudden fixation. "You don't even know him."

The man, himself, had to be even more foolish to write a girl such a note. If she were to report the note, he would be fired, immediately, perhaps even jailed.

"I'm going to do it, Isabel. Will you help me?"

My own driver waved to me from behind a throng of green-uniformed girls. I waved back.

"Of course not," I said. "Promise me you won't do it?"

We watched the driver climb into his seat. The orange bus set loose a sand storm as he backed it out of the parking lot. "I want to see what he wants," Laila said.

"We know what he wants."

"What?" Laila goaded me.

I was embarrassed. "I-I guess he wants to kiss you or something."

"Yes," she said, "he probably wants to kiss me."

"But, he's married."

"So?"

"You don't care?"

She shrugged, puckering her lips slightly. "I feel like being kissed. It doesn't matter whether or not he's married. If he doesn't care, why should I?"

99

This particular hedonism that always seemed to propel Laila, along with the sudden, puzzling, eagerness to be kissed, amazed me.

"Have you ever kissed anyone? Any man?" I asked.

"Only my father—and my brother. But that's different."

"You aren't scared? I mean, it can't be much fun."

"I'm not scared at all."

Kissing and sex were still mysteries to me, bringing back only shreds of memories of the moist, slightly unpleasant mouths of the boys' with whom we used to play 'spin the bottle'. Notwithstanding my attraction to Saqr last year, kissing boys or men seemed to be without any obvious benefit or pleasure. I did not understand why Laila was so bent on exposing herself to such a ridiculous, dangerous experiment with a complete stranger, even if he was the best looking man that we were apt to encounter on the school grounds.

But my hesitancy only inflamed Laila. "You want to know what it's like, don't you?" she asked, her eyes flashing. "Well, now we'll know."

Perhaps it was the lure of the dangerous—defying her parents and the school's tyrannical teachers—rather than the actual kiss that intrigued her. Laila's pouting lips did not fool me as easily as she thought, and I did not believe that they hungered for this man's lips or anyone else's. However, I agreed to help her keep the secret rendezvous—for the sake of knowledge.

One logistical detail remained to be worked out and that was how to get Laila to school by seven o'clock when her bus did not normally arrive there until eight.

It was certainly too far to walk to Fahaheel from Shuaiba and there were no taxis readily available. To ask my driver to pick us both up that early would raise suspicion at home. I briefly entertained the idea of riding Noor to Shuaiba early Thursday morning and picking Laila up. It would take around an hour for us to get to Fahaheel at a reasonable pace. However, two girls on a horse in Fahaheel would be outrageously conspicuous and there was no place to leave Noor during the day when we were in class and no way to explain this unusual request to my parents.

As usual, Laila resolved this detail. We would simply tell our respective parents that we would be spending the night at a friend's house to study for an exam and actually sleep at school.

"Sleep here?"

"Why not?" Laila asked, excited, "we'll sleep in the infirmary or in the janitor's quarters."

"How will we get in? Aren't the rooms locked each afternoon?"

"We'll hide inside and they can lock us in."

"How will we get out? They don't reopen them before seven o'clock."

"Then," Laila said, no doubt realizing that the kiss would have to take place sometime between 6:45 when the bus drivers arrived at school and 7:15 when they started their bus routes, "there's only one thing to do. We'll stay after school and sleep on the bus."

At some point I again asked Laila why she was doing this, why we were so meticulously planning this outrageous experiment. For, more and more, I was beginning to see this hunting for a kiss as nothing more than a risky foray into territory where we did not yet belong.

"Isabel," she said, finally, taking a breath as though preparing me for a great blow, "we must do the best with what we've got. If I am beautiful, then I am meant to be admired and kissed by men. It's my destiny. I'm not saying that everyone should. It might even be wrong for some. Besides," she added, trying to reassure me, "my mother says that in love there is no shame."

101

17

"In love there is no shame," the woman in the dream said with a flick of her molasses curls. Yet even in the dream, I could hardly believe that Laila's mother was telling her daughter such a thing. Her lush, open lips seemed to quiver as she said it, as though she were considering the impact of her words, wondering whether she should add anything to qualify her statement. In real life, she must have been talking to someone else when Laila overheard her—an enraged husband, perhaps, or an indignant neighbor woman. Of two things I was certain: she said it proudly, and it was not intended for children's ears—especially not for those of her daughter, Laila.

During the last five years, ever since the death of her baby, Bilal, I had seen Laila's mother undergo a profound change. Her girlish face now had an unsettled look, as though at any moment the pretty, loose features would contort into a sharp, unpredictable tangle of nose, kohl-smeared eyes, and red mouth as they succumbed to rage or tears.

She, now, apparently, spent much of her time alone during the day except for when she visited another Lebanese woman down the road. Most of her Kuwaiti neighbors in Shuaiba kept to themselves behind the ornate wooden doors of their court-yards, tending their children and preparing the food that their husbands or sons bought at the market for the main, mid-day meal. Although the Lebanese women were not disliked, the traditional Kuwaiti women of Shuaiba did not comprehend their lack of shame in baring their arms and legs outside their homes. They must also have wondered about the painted, graven images on the walls of these women's homes, knowing that such images of animals and humans were an affront to Islam. After a few attempts at being friendly when Laila's family had first moved in, the Kuwaiti women had gone back to their own private lives behind their doors, mixing only among themselves.

Laila's mother was still cheerful whenever I was at her house or whenever she paid my mother a courtesy call which she faithfully did once every few months since the day of the fire when my mother showed up at her doorstep with the blankets and the cake. Yet, she also seemed nervous, mumbling to her-self in her kitchen or sitting room when she thought no one saw her or frowning as she fussed with her hair or dress as she opened the door for Laila's father and one of the men he sometimes brought home.

Although I had witnessed this myself several times—Laila's mother accompanying some well-dressed man into the back of the house for a half hour or so, emerging later looking flushed and tired—not a word had ever passed between Laila and my-self on the subject.

Perhaps it was after one such session, after one such guest had left the house, that her mother confronted someone with the determined phrase that Laila had overheard: "In love there is no shame."

In my dream on the bus that night, an endless, humid night that seemed to linger on minute by minute just to spite Laila

103

and myself for having deceived our parents, I heard Laila's mother laugh as she used to before Bilal's death and say, "In love there is no shame."

When I opened my eyes, Laila was already awake and staring into the bus's rearview mirror as she thrashed a comb through her newly-cut short, black hair. My watch showed 6:15. The sky still glowed with the pink patina of dawn, but the sun was already bright, the heat seeping into the bus through cracks in the windows. I watched Laila a moment from the back row of seats where I was stretched out, trying to remember where I was, finally having fallen asleep on the sticky vinyl and wishing more than ever that I was actually at Basima's house where I had told my parents I would be.

I patted the wrinkles of my bunched, green-check summer uniform, wondering how to explain my disheveled appearance later at school. Then I heard the crunching of tires across the sand of the school parking lot...

Laila looked away from the mirror, her lower lip dropping.

"Oh, God," I said, recognizing in the small car, below, the young man's red T-shirt. "What are we going to do?"

"Is he alone?" Laila whispered.

"Did you expect his wife and baby?" I was suddenly frightened, hating myself for having gone along with this plan.

She glanced at her face in the mirror a last time. "Don't worry. You stay on the bus. I'll be back," she said. Then, she slid open the bus door and hopped down the steps.

I watched, horrified, as she disappeared, as though once the sand enveloped her she would be gone forever or else regurgitated back as something unrecognizable!

I went to the front of the bus and looked out. No one was in sight. I jumped down the steps, myself, just missing a wriggling black snake with a yellow neck. I backed away, watching it slither under the bus, its skin glittering like diamond chips. All

104

at once, I remembered something the Kuwaiti girls said at school—that black snakes with yellow collars always brought good luck.

I walked to the back end of the bus and peered around it. Then I went from bus to bus. Laila was nowhere to be seen.

The bus driver's small, empty car was parked against the school wall, and the blue school gate was open. I assumed that Laila and the driver were inside. I hesitated, then headed for the gate, afraid of what I might see and yet determined to protect Laila from harm if she needed me.

Inside the gate, again, there was no one. The school had a docile, tranquil appearance in the absence of the stern authority of the teachers who were probably still upstairs in their quarters. It could have been a museum or a park with its vast, sandy grounds, scattered water fountains, and trellised corridors. I enjoyed the idea of a park which momentarily dissipated my fear of being found by one of the teachers. I closed my eyes, listening to the birds perched on the trellises.

Then, someone grabbed me. I opened my eyes. It was the bus driver, his hand clamp over my burning wrist.

I smelled sweat, an acrid, manly smell combined with a sweet scent of palm oil from his hair. I stared at him, at his unflinching dark eyes, the mustache.

"What are you doing here?" he hissed.

I opened my mouth to cry out, then stopped.

"Who are you?" he asked, relaxing his grip a bit.

"I—I came with Laila."

"Laila?"

"Yes."

"Laila?" he asked, again.

"Laila. You were to meet her here."

The bus driver dropped my wrist. I stood and simply stared at him because my legs would not move. They seemed fixed in

105

the sand. I was afraid to call for help, yet equally afraid of being touched again by this stranger.

He, too, stared at me without a word, as though trying to make up his mind what to think of me, of my unwashed face and loose ponytail, my pale eyes, my freckles which he seemed to be counting one by one.

He took a step toward me. I stood, waiting for whatever would happen, watching him hesitate a moment before slowly lowering his head, his breath scarring my cheek, until his warm mouth touched mine. I did not move away or make a sound when his lips tugged at mine, only waited for him to finish, imagining Laila whispering, "In love there is no shame."

I did pull back, finally, realizing that I had just been kissed my a man and remembering my own notion that sex was vaguely violent and unpleasant. I pushed the driver away, wiped my mouth, and pressing my skirt pocket against my thigh to keep in the pens and erasers that jingled as I ran, I fled out through the school gate.

Although the driver made no attempt to restrain me, I felt that he had enjoyed kissing me. Somehow, in the end, this seemed important.

Laila stood at the bus door looking visibly shaken. Her eyes narrowed when she saw me running toward her.

"Where have you been?" she demanded.

"Looking for you," I said, catching my breath. "Where have *you* been?"

"I thought you were going to wait here for me."

"I was worried about you," I said, feeling that she could read every line on my face, every pore, and knew that I was lying to her.

Instead of reprimanding me, though, she lowered her eyes and the familiar smirk appeared.

"I got scared and hid in the watchman's room," she said.

106

"You *what?*" I shouted. "what about the driver?"

"I don't know. I didn't see him."

"But we waited all night. You mean we did all this for nothing?"

Laila looked annoyed, impatient. "What's wrong with you, Isabel? This had nothing to do with you."

"Nothing to do with me? You wanted me to be with you. You *asked* me to. We went through all this for nothing!"

"Not for nothing. It just wasn't the right time. Someday you'll know what I mean."

"You talk too much, Laila," I said, tears filling my eyes.

Suddenly the night's sleeplessness, the fear, the guilt of lying to our parents, and finally my first kiss—totally unplanned—were too much for me. I felt like a small, lost child and wanted to go home to my room, my horse, my mother's safe arms.

But it was Laila who embraced me, instead, looking frightened and shaken by my hysterical outburst.

Patting my back, she crooned "Don't cry, Isabel. Someday you'll understand. There is no shame in love, really there isn't. Someday you'll understand."

18

It was December of the following year. There had been unusually good rains and the desert was unseasonably coated with
a fuzzy layer of green grass. The coveted dandelions, the desert's
first signs of spring, sprouted in yellow patches amidst currents
of tiny blue irises as though it were already March. Carloads of
Kuwaitis from the city began to appear in the desert in larger
and larger numbers on Fridays, as they always did much later in
the spring, in the camp-outs that freed them temporarily from
urban life and served as a ritual reminder of their bedouin
past. Even tribesmen from Iraq and Saudi Arabia with their
animals could be seen drifting across the borders to take advan-
tage of the greening, Kuwait desert.

It was right before Christmas that I learned that Saqr was in
England. I learned this from Andrea Deer who saw him on the
airplane coming home for Christmas vacation. The last time I

had seen him was that summer day over a year ago at the examination center in the city. Since then, more than a year of high school had passed for me, a year of college for him.

"Are you still friendly with that boy—you know, that local?" Andrea asked me when we met going into the compound club to watch one of the English films shown several times a week. "What was his name?"

"We never were friendly, Andrea," I said, bristling at her use of the word, 'local'. It was the same way I had heard countless British and American people refer to Kuwaitis, as if they meant to say, *coolie.*

"Well, that night at my house he seemed to have had eyes only for you," she said.

"That was two years ago," I said, dismissing the compliment, yet elated despite myself that she still remembered that Saqr had barely talked to anyone else that night.

"He was on the same flight as me over from London. He says he's at Cambridge. He asked about you, asked how long I had known you. He's quite nice—said he wants to see you while he's here. I told him you went to school in Fahaheel."

I turned to face her, my heart suddenly racing. "Why did you tell him I go to Fahaheel?"

"Aren't you still there?"

"Yes, but you shouldn't have told him."

"Why not?" Andrea looked surprised by my anger. "He said he wanted to see you."

In all the years that Andrea had lived in Kuwait, she seemed not to have learned much about Arabs. Fresh from London, she seemed to think it perfectly natural for a boy and girl to get together whenever they felt like it. It was even desirable, something as normal as eating or drinking, something that was not in the least bit complicated. Yet, how could she have assumed that for me it would be that simple? How could she not know that to be seen with a boy—especially one like Saqr who had earned a certain reputation merely by being a bin Ahmad and being the son of his father—would have severe consequences?

My mother had kept the Christmas traditions in our home each year and even my father, a Muslim, enthusiastically joined in trimming the Christmas tree and exchanging gifts with the other Arab Christians and expatriates in our compound. Although my teachers had grown accustomed to my absence from school for two days during the festivities, the Fahaheel school did not let out except New Years Day, and thus it was at the congested school gate on the day after Christmas, as girls were shouting and waving to each other as they boarded the buses, that I spotted Saqr.

He was standing across the school parking lot next to a low, silver sports car. I realized that I had felt something pulling me in his direction, the direction from which a light breeze was blowing, as if he had sent me some curious, silent summons.

He was wearing a gray, winter *dishdasha* and a red and white checkered headdress that gently flapped in the breeze like the wings of a stingray. He seemed to be firmly planted in the sand, although I kept imagining that he might disappear if I looked at him for too long.

He did not wave to me so as not to attract attention and, without thinking, I sent my driver home, saying that I would be spending the afternoon with a friend. When the disgruntled driver left, I mustered up the courage to walk toward Saqr.

It seemed to take an eternity to cross the school parking lot, the sand scoured by busses' tire tracks and soaked by the recent rains that, besides the blooming flowers, had left huge puddles of mud that had dried into broken, chocolate-like chunks. The cool, dry breeze blew through my woolen uniform, causing my skin to itch and harden.

As I drew closer to him, forgetting the sounds of the motors and the chattering voices behind me, avoiding any astonished glances from the girls that might have been cast my way, it

110

suddenly occurred to me that Saqr might be waiting for someone else! Perhaps he knew one of the other girls—one of the
Kuwaitis with charcoal hair as straight and thick as a horse's
mane, and brown, almond eyes; a girl whose skin was the ripe,
mellow color of oiled wood. For one awful moment, I even
thought that he might have been waiting for Laila.

Then, he smiled, as though my strolling toward him amused
him, made him happy, smiled as though we had seen each
other only yesterday. I knew, then, that he was there for me.

"Isabel?"

He always asked it, as though never quite sure it was me.

"I think I remember you," I said.

"I think I remember you, too" he said, his eyes at once narrowing and twinkling.

"How long has it been?"

"You've grown up," he said.

"You shouldn't have come. My school, my friends...I have to
be careful."

"How have you been?" he asked, as though he had not heard
my reproach, was oblivious to my concerns. When he spoke, his
mouth relaxed into a wide grin, his white teeth lighting up his
dark skin.

Once the girls had all left the parking lot, we sat in his car.
We were still sitting in his car, talking, when the sun began to
set, its orange glow lifting off the horizon and invading the
entire breadth of the sky. We only talked, never once touching,
not even holding hands. I knew that I had to content myself
with being in his sphere, within his reach, ignoring the cruel
yearnings of my body and heart.

Saqr did most of the talking, in his new, British accent, as
though purging himself of his past, needing me to understand
him as fully as possible.

He told me about his father's bedouin ancestors who had
become traders at the turn of the century in the early days of
Kuwait. In the early 1800s, his family had gained control of the

boat-building business and owned a fleet of some 100 ships that both fished and exported pearls, dates, fish, sheep, wool, hides, skins, and horses in addition to hauling in the vital boatloads of sweet, drinking water from Iraq. Most of the men in his family became traders in the last century and it was during their long travels across the Gulf to Iran that some began to marry into Iranian families. He told me that his mother's family still lived in Shiraz. Yet the Persian influence in Kuwait was very old, he said. In 1776, the Persians had captured Basra in Iraq. Since Kuwait was the chief outlet on the Gulf of Mesopotamea, much of the present Persian population of the city, including some members of his mother's family, was a remnant of this occupation.

Then he told me stories of his father's family, Kuwaiti bedouins. In the old tribal wars, he said, it had been the custom to set a virgin girl in a litter on a camel's back at a point beyond which the enemy was not to pass. Being defenseless, the girl symbolized the tribe's honor, spurring the men on to fight to the death to protect her. Many battles over grazing grounds, animals, and belongings were won that way, he said.

He talked, too, of his parents' marriage, how on their wedding night his father had cut his own thumb to produce the required bride's blood on the wedding sheets because his mother had been too young and too frightened to let her groom come near her.

He seemed to relish the surprise I could not hide at his frank conversation, and at how different his family was from that of my friends, and so very different from my own. I think that I was even more astonished, however, by his knowledge of history, by his ability not only to recite facts but to talk of these remote events as though they were his own current, personal experiences.

"Am I truly the first person to tell you that you are beautiful?" he said, suddenly, turning to me.

Without thinking, I nodded, then immediately wished I had not.

"The first time a woman told me that I was beautiful, I was thirteen," he said softly, still looking right at me. "Then, she took me to bed."

As he recounted all this—the story of the chaste virgins on camels, of his father's sensitivity toward his young bride, of his own seduction at thirteen—I sensed that he was really wanting to tell me something else.

Stifled by his frankness, I tried to change the subject. "What's it like at Cambridge?"

"Cambridge?"

"Isn't that where you are now?"

"How did you know?" he asked, looking surprised.

"What are you studying?"

"Law."

"Law?" I was impressed. "Is it interesting?"

"I study all night and we row during the day. There's a river through the college. In the afternoons we have tea. They serve a lot of tea in England," he said, as though puzzled, "but never with mint."

"Is it hard?" I asked.

"Studies?"

"Being away from home, from the desert."

He followed my sweeping gesture, looking at the sand of the empty school parking lot, at the lights encircling the tip of the minaret on a mosque down the road, at the red sky. "Yes, it's hard."

"But you like it?"

"It's all right," he said, shrugging. "I have my friends."

"The same ones from here?"

He smiled. "The same."

"Any girlfriends?"

This time he looked surprised by my candor. He lay his head back on the seat and closed his eyes. "A few."

"English?" I ventured.

He did not answer. "What have *you* been doing for a whole

113

year?" he asked, abruptly starting the car engine.

I knew that I should not have pried into his affairs, but I was annoyed that he so readily admitted to liking other girls, as though I had no feelings.

"You can't take me home," I said, turning to him, staring at his broad jaw, at the dark hair just below the skin. His nose was curved, more Iranian than Kuwaiti. Oddly, in profile, his face did not have the same charm as when he looked straight at me. "You'll have to take me to my friend's house in Shuaiba. I'll show you how to get there."

"I know Shuaiba," he said, his foot pressing down on the pedal. The car lunged forward and I felt suddenly free, as though for a brief, few moments, I was in control of my destiny. Before we were out of the parking lot, he swerved and we went round and round in a circle, creating considerable commotion and a curtain of dust around us.

Then he suddenly pressed on the brake, switched off the motor, pulled my head toward him, and kissed me.

His closed eyelids and lashes against his dark skin made him seem as vulnerable as a baby. I watched as he kissed me, afraid to lose him if I closed my own eyes. It was the second time that a man's lips touched mine in the unexpected demand of a kiss. For the second time, I was not sure that I liked this wet, awkward exchange.

But I knew that I liked Saqr, knew that he made me feel beautiful in a way no other person ever had, and I forced myself to stop resisting and to concentrate on what was happening. His lips brushing against my cheek, moving up and down my neck, were softer than I thought any man's lips could be. I reached around his neck and pulled him closer, my hands grasping him. I was finally in Saqr's arms where I had dreamed of being for so long. He said something into my ear—I love you, perhaps—and my breasts hardened like stone.

Then, all at once, Saqr's hand sank between my knees. I stiffened and clamped my legs shut.

114

Now, I was frightened and disappointed. "We had better go," I said, angry that he had cut short my serenity.

He leaned back in the seat, his eyes closed, breathing as though he had just run a marathon. Without a word, he restarted the engine. I sat still, my heart flying, trying to recapture the memory of his body against mine, of his breaths in mine, of what might have happened if I had not stopped him. As we drove across the darkened desert to Shuaiba, to Laila's house, I tried not to think that I might never feel his kisses again.

"Well, what do you think about kissing, now?" Laila whispered, intrigued, as I waited for my father to pick me up from her house. I had just finished telling her about the afternoon with Saqr. In response to her questions, I rolled my eyes and smiled knowingly, the way that I had seen the British and American girls do when they talked about their boyfriends.

"That good?" she asked.

"That *wonderful*," I corrected her, stretching, and suddenly sleepy.

"Isabel had her first kiss," she said, amused, as though it were hardly believable.

I smiled. I had never informed her of the episode with the bus driver the year before. Anyway, this was the sort of kiss that truly counted.

"And with the boy of your dreams," she went on.

I smiled.

"And he loves you?"

I looked at her, surprised. "I don't know."

"How could he not love our adorable Isabel?" she said, her eyes as sharp as steel.

It was an odd thing for her to say, and yet I believed her as the memory of the afternoon returned in all of its sweetness. I closed my eyes, and suddenly could still inhale the scent of

115

Saqr's skin, that singular flavor of incense and musk that had always seemed to linger about him. I could still feel his hands on my face, drawing me to his lips.

Suddenly, Laila said, "I doubt that you're a virgin, though."

I opened my eyes. "What?"

"I'm not talking about today."

"What, then?"

"It's all your horseback riding. It does away with virginity."

"Who told you that?" I said, angrily.

"Everybody knows it. Why do you think my mother never allows me to ride?"

"That's ridiculous." I was furious with her for being envious, for taking this afternoon away from me.

She smiled, tilting her head. "It's true."

"It's not true. And, anyway, who cares?"

"Obviously, *he* cares. Why else would he tell you about his parents' wedding night? He was trying to find out whether or not you're a virgin. He would want a virgin."

"Well, I am."

Laila shrugged.

"I *am*," I insisted.

Later, I could not get to sleep, thinking about what Laila had said. My dreams were intermittently interrupted by images of things red—my mother's blood-red zinnias, the red of Laila's mother's lipstick, my red hair. Those blood dreams assaulted me relentlessly until I had to get up for school the next morning, wondering how to find out whether or not I was still a virgin.

LAILA

19

I suppose I was, in a childish way, a little in love with Isabel myself, and hearing about her new-found suitor made me feel ridiculously like a repudiated lover. I felt suddenly abandoned, a void welling within me that I had not felt since my grandmother's death. I knew that I had to put a dent in her happiness, somehow.

In truth, I found all this concern over virginity silly, although I could tell from Isabel's wild eyes and pursed lips that she did not. I had startled her into thought. She wanted to be a virgin—had to be—for him, for this Saqr bin Ahmad. Seeing her so radiant, so completely transformed by a man, forced me to plant that seed of doubt in her.

We had been taught that we had to remain pure, remain *girls*, until we married. That, in itself, was not so difficult since many girls were married off as soon as they reached their teens. Even skinny Aisha Rashid, married before sixth grade, already had two children. Isabel and I, at fifteen, were of the new generation of girls who were opting for school rather than marriage.

The complex workings of the female body had naturally absorbed us these past few years and the subject of sex, which had been a taboo topic of discussion to us when we were younger, was of great interest to us in high school. Frequently, we talked of menstruation and even of sexual intercourse, although the possibility of any of us not being virgins never entered our minds.

Despite all this emphasis on chastity, unlike the other girls, I managed to maintain a perspective which refused to take it too seriously.

This probably had to do with Aida.

Some years after we had settled in Shuaiba, after the birth of Bilal and the added strain on our family finances—my father had yet to strike it rich—I became aware of the nature of the visitations by the men who occasionally came home with my father after work. Sameer had shouted it out to me once, in anger. Yet I had done some thinking on my own even before that incident. I knew and yet I did not know of the relationship between these men and my mother. I believed and yet I refused to believe.

I also knew, even then, that it had to do with money. A welder's pay did not go far and we needed food, clothing, and a roof over our heads. Each time that I received a new dress or toy, I assumed that the benevolent source was Aida.

At first I was shocked by the transactions that occurred right under my father's nose and, apparently, with his approval. Whenever a man would come in Sameer's presence and my brother would glare at me as though I were the cause of all this, I became filled with hatred for Aida. For all I knew, in fact, it could have been during such an episode that I was conceived, destined to be separated from everyone in the family, including my own mother, forever.

Then, as I grew older and came to sense the secret fear Aida harbored, that her husband would one day grow insane like his brother, Issa, had in Lebanon, I felt that perhaps her actions had less to do with money than self-preservation. Perhaps, in some strange way, Aida was indirectly searching for some way to keep herself from ever becoming too dependent on my father. She used her body not only to help us, but to preserve her own freedom.

Eventually, I became indifferent to it all.

ISABEL

20

"Isabel, are you still here?" my mother says, looking up from her cards as I tiptoe from the hall into the dark living room.

"I'm going soon," I say, peering out the glass doors to the street leading up to the club. The street forms a sort of large horseshoe so that a car's lights can be seen bobbing through the desert from a long way off. Nothing resembling Laila's little MG has shown itself.

"I thought you'd already gone," she replies, her voice trailing, distracted, her concern directed more to the card game than to my still being here.

She puts down a card carefully, thoughtfully, to the obvious dissatisfaction of my father, who lets out a yelp of protest. My mother, as sharp as she is in so many things, has no talent for cards. She once won the prize for lowest score at a bridge club luncheon.

"Is something wrong?" she says to me.

"Laila's late," I tell her.

"Where is she?"

"I don't know."

"I hope nothing's happened," my mother says, her voice trailing. There is the soft snap of her putting down another card.

"What's going to happen?" I ask, irritably.

"Strategy," my father interjects, brusquely. "How often do I have to teach you strategy? How can you put down your *queen* now?"

"Why not?" my mother asks, sounding genuinely bewildered.

"Because the *king* hasn't been discarded yet. Have you been paying attention?"

"Of course the king has been discarded," my mother retorts.

"I have the king," my father says, calmly.

I go back down the hall to my bedroom, hearing my parents' quibbling voices even after I have closed my door.

I suddenly remember lying in my bed as a child after being tucked in at night, listening to the soothing duet of their voices in the living room down the hall as I drifted off to sleep. Their voices seemed to stretch on forever on those nights, as though they would surely live forever, never dying, never leaving me.

On other nights in those early years, just as I fell asleep, I would suddenly be confronted by something dark and terrifying in my bedroom, a tall, unfamiliar man standing at my closet. I would try to run out to my parents as they sat chatting in the living room, calling out to them for help, but I could neither move nor make any sound come out of my mouth.

That paralyzing nightmare recurred so often that I came to know beforehand that it was useless to try to call out and pushed my sleeping brain to devise an alternative strategy of waking myself as soon as the dream started. On one occasion, however, I actually walked into my dark bedroom to find the tall, shadowy figure of my dreams hovering before the closet as if waiting for me. As in my dreams, I stood unable to move, hardly believing that my worst fears had come true. Then I realized that it

126

was only my father standing there, searching for something in my closet.

Years later, the intruder in my dream took on a different identity. More and more he grew to resemble Saqr. Yet whenever I got close enough to see his profile the man would disappear, proving to be as illusive as all the other figures who had stood before my closet all those years.

Shortly before we moved to the Fahaheel school, a new mosque was built in our compound near the refinery. It had green-painted cement walls and an extravagant gold dome and minaret. Five times a day—at dawn, noon, afternoon, evening, and night—the *mu'athin* who had been hired to recite would climb to the top of the slender minaret and call out the prayers for the Muslim employees, his voice emanating from the summit while the bright flare of the refinery burned atop the tall pipe behind him.

The blind, portly *mu'athin* lived with his wife, daughter, and three little boys in modest quarters adjacent to the mosque. His daughter was my age, round-faced and plump like her father yet pretty in a delicate way like her diminutive, bird-faced mother. Her name, Sahaab, or Cloud, aptly described her absent-minded nature.

Since Sahaab went to my school in Fahaheel, it was arranged that the driver would stop by the mosque each morning after picking me up to pick her up. After so many years of silent rides to and from school each day, her company was both a welcome change and an intrusion, an inhibitor of the fantasies and daydreams that had become such a natural, even an essential, part of the fifteen-minute morning and afternoon drives.

The *mu'athin* and his wife were Syrians from Damascus. Sahaab's pale, round face was bland except for her pronounced cheekbones. Her blond hair was as straight as the desert camel grass and she had uncommonly strong, white teeth.

127

Unfortunately, she also seemed somewhat dim and was constantly chastised by the teachers for not responding to their questions quickly enough or for not having understood the lessons; she was chided by the girls, themselves, for her dull good-naturedness. From the start, she attached herself to me with a docile loyalty that both flattered and annoyed me since I knew I could not return it equally. Yet, I felt an amicable tolerance towards her since she was the only other girl my age left in the compound by then. In the afternoons, after school, I often rode my bike the half mile from our house to the mosque to visit her.

It was odd to have a friend who practically lived in a mosque. The first time that I visited, her father agreed to take us up to the encircling balcony of the minaret to see where he stood with his megaphone to call out the *athan*.

He unlocked a small door on one side of the mosque, and we followed him up the winding concrete steps. Sahaab's three small brothers raced ahead of Sahaab and me as we climbed the wedged, unlit, spiral steps. Sensing my way up each step with the tip of my shoe, groping for the walls on either side, I followed the tap-tapping of the father's cane ahead of us, imagining myself climbing to the top of a tower to rescue some forsaken princess.

Finally, as a crack of light appeared above us and we surfaced into the open air, it seemed as if we were suddenly face to face with God!

It was dizzying to be so high, to stand in the spot from which the *mu'athin* called out God's words. The air seemed thinner and lighter up there with no dust or sand to cloud it. There was a commanding view of the entire compound—the pastel houses lined up one next to the other along the beach, the club with its open-air theater and tennis courts, the stables, the clinic, the employees' mess hall, the flags marking the various holes of the new golf course which had been marked out in the surrounding desert, and, finally, the refinery and flare behind us.

Descending the stairs after that breathtaking height seemed to take forever. Several times I stopped, my legs locked in fear that I would lose my footing and slip down into the blackness.

The morning following my unplanned meeting with Saqr, Sahaab confronted me in the car on the way to school.

"You didn't come home with us yesterday."

"I went home with Laila."

"You should be careful," she said, softly, turning her head slightly to shield her words from the driver in the front.

"Careful of what?" I said, irritated that she would probe into my affairs.

"People will talk. Someone could tell on you."

"What are you talking about?"

"I saw you get into the car with that man yesterday. Someone might tell your father," she said.

"Then, let them tell." Realizing, suddenly, that this was just the way that Laila would have responded to such a warning, I chuckled. She would be pleased by my challenging anyone trying to interfere with my life.

But Sahaab's placid brow wrinkled. "My father would kill me if I did such a thing."

"He wouldn't."

"Doesn't your father beat you?"

"Of course not. Does your father beat you?"

She nodded. "Sometimes. He beats my brothers and my mother, too."

I was embarrassed and shocked by this sudden, unsolicited revelation. Sahaab's father was the *Mu'athin*, after all. He was blind and helpless, negotiating the world through the tip of his cane with a perpetual placid grin on his round face which was never free of gray stubble. That such a man would inspire anything but pity, especially in his daughter, surprised me.

Yet, Sahaab's mother, a tiny woman with a fragile, bony face shyly confirmed her daughter's words one afternoon. She seemed even more hopelessly simple than Sahaab, never raising her voice at her three devilish sons except to whine at them in desperation. Although she was young enough to be her husband's daughter, to be Sahaab's sister, she seemed used up; spent and empty.

Whenever I went there, her mother sat with us in the tiny, spare foyer and served us tea and anisette cookies. Never having been to school herself, she would listen in apt wonder as Sahaab and I discussed the day's events in Fahaheel, often peppering our conversation with scandalous stories we had heard from the other girls. She would latch on to our every word, leaving us only long enough to make quick forays into the other room whenever her husband called her for something.

To Sahaab, my getting into Saqr's car must have seemed like the action of someone from another planet. Because she, herself, was in no way awakened to the concept of romance, she did not understand nor need the sublime delight of it. She was still a child in this regard, shielded from films and books about it. I could not imagine her dreaming of love as I did. Nor could I see her being driven, as Laila was, to investigate the possibilities of her body, such as kissing. She seemed to have no idea, in fact, of those possibilities.

Occasionally, Sahaab's mother paid my mother an afternoon call. She would appear at our door, having walked all the way from the mosque across the sand dunes with Sahaab and her three boys. She would smile her puzzled smile and enter our house as confidently as if she had been invited. My mother, who usually sequestered herself away in her room in the afternoons to read the latest books that had been sent to her by friends in New York, would dutifully get up to greet this peculiar, unbidden guest.

As with Laila's mother's visits, the conversation was conducted in a melange of English, Arabic, and sign language. My mother's Arabic was not good but since Laila's mother was quick to catch on and painted her own speech with an array of gestures, she and my mother found much to talk about. Sahaab's mother, on the other hand, spoke no English and seemed to misinterpret much of what my mother said. She would turn to Sahaab or to me and whisper, "What did she say?" after practically every sentence, while her boys jumped up and down at her feet, flinging each other onto the floor and narrowly missing the table with the tea things.

My mother never let on to me, however, that she found those meetings trying, nor would she stop buying Sahaab and her brothers gifts at Christmas time—despite my warnings that the boys would get into trouble with their father because they were beginning to prefer Christmas over the Muslim *Eid* when they received only a bit of spending money and a new suit of clothes.

21

The Kuwaiti girls said that the pure of heart, those who neither envied anyone nor cast the evil eye, possessed the sixth sense. They also said that one who truly believed in God could foresee one's own death.

The purest person I knew was Sahaab. Perhaps this was an innate part of her or perhaps it was the poverty that she and her family had endured for so long which had chiseled away any meanness. Whatever the reason for her evident good nature, her telling me that I should not see Saqr any more began to seem like a genuine harbinger of misfortune, although it was something much more than my parents' anger that I feared.

On the other hand, I was pleased to discover that some part of me did not care what anyone thought, that I was becoming more like Laila, defiant, selfish, pleasure-seeking.

"Rubbish," Laila said when I told her of Sahaab's warning.

"But she knows something. I can see it in her eyes. She has the sight," I insisted.

"Cow's eyes! She can't see any more than can that horrid father of hers."

"How can you make fun of a blind man? That's not the kind of sight I'm talking about."

"Whatever you're talking about I can tell you that she doesn't have it. She's just trying to scare you," Laila quipped.

"You know what they say about purity. Her father's the *mu'athin*."

"*Mu'athin*? He doesn't know the first thing about purity. Just look at the way he treats Sahaab and her mother. Like slaves."

I did not contradict Laila, but her words did not comfort me, either. Sahaab's warning still rang in my ears.

"What does Sahaab tell you, anyway? That loving is wrong? How would she know?"

"She didn't say that loving is wrong."

"Then what did she say?"

"She said that Saqr would never love me."

"And how does she know that?"

"It's just the way she says it. She scares me."

"Well, if you believe that, you're as dumb as she is," Laila snapped.

I suddenly wished that I had not told Laila any of this. I felt like a fool and a coward. She was clearly disappointed in me.

"Tell me something," she said, matter-of-fact, as she did whenever she wanted to extract some vital piece of information from someone. "What does Sahaab tell you about me? Has she any predictions for me?"

"Why would she talk about you?"

"I'm just asking."

"She hasn't said anything about you," I said, or rather lied, for Sahaab had warned me more than once that Laila's end would not be a good one. I usually ignored what she said about my friend who was, after all, Sahaab's antithesis and one of the girls who tormented her the most.

133

Despite Laila's reassurance, I, myself, was not entirely blind to the nature of Saqr's interest in me. Although I knew that he found me appealing, I worried that he wanted me merely because I was like the girl on the camel: chaste, vulnerable, and above all, unattainable. In a sense I *was* unattainable compared with the European or American girls he could easily have gone out with. But I also knew that as far as any deeper commitment was concerned, he was not ready. The only sort of relationship that would be permitted by my family, on the other hand, was one that would eventually lead to marriage. As for him, his family would probably not permit him to consider a girl who was not a bin Ahmad, someone they had not hand-picked themselves.

Although I rarely saw Saqr now that he was in England for most of the year, he continued to pervade my life like some restive phantom. One such time was in Spring, right after my sixteenth birthday.

It had been a disappointing birthday, not at all the cornerstone of my growing up that I had anticipated. Surprisingly, nothing about me had changed by the arrival of this long-awaited number. I did not feel a shred different from the day before, despite my mother's gift of a fluffy, nylon nightgown to acknowledge my budding womanhood, and despite the fact that Mrs. Deer, Andrea's mother, had come over to give me a box of embroidered, Chinese handkerchiefs to cry into.

The nightgown blew about my body like air, weightless as butterfly wings, revealing my breasts underneath. It was my first such nightgown and I wore it to bed every night.

On one of these nights, while my parents were out, I was surprised by a telephone call from Saqr.

"How did you get my number?" I said.

"I can find out anything I want to about you," he said. My heart began to pound as it did whenever I saw him or heard his voice, as though he could see into my soul and read my every feeling.

"I thought you'd gone back to Cambridge," I said, not having seen him since that afternoon at school in December.

"I'm leaving in the morning."

I waited for him to say something, either that he missed me or that he did not want to leave for England. The thought of his leaving without my seeing him already stung me.

Instead he said, "I want to come and see you."

I was silent.

"May I?"

"When?"

"Now," he said, softly.

"You can't come now."

"Why not?"

"Because my parents aren't here."

"You're alone?"

"Yes," I said.

"Then I'm coming. I'm not far from you. I'm at our beach house."

The Tower...the thought of him being so close made me almost give in. I had ridden Noor there several days earlier but the place had looked deserted, as though no one had used it in a long time. The white, decorative paint around the windows was peeling and some of the jutting plaster work had broken off the ramparts. A side flank of a mud wall facing the sea had caved in, probably from the winter storm some months back.

"No," I said, annoyed at him for teasing me, for always making me push him away. "I'm going to bed."

"What are you wearing?" he asked.

"Why?"

"I miss you."

"I'm wearing a nightgown," I said, flatly, knowing that to say so was foolish, yet somehow hoping that it might magically make him come crashing through the glass doors of the patio.

135

"A nightgown?" he hesitated, as though surprised that I would say this. Then, obviously emboldened, his voice grew more direct, "Is it white?"

"No."

"What color is it?"

"It's pink."

"Pink? Then you must be waiting for me."

"Saqr?" I said, boldly.

"Yes?"

"Are you alone?"

"Why?"

"Are your friends there with you, the ones you're always with?"

He laughed, hesitating a moment. "Of course not."

I strained to hear any voices in the background in case I might simply be the target of some masculine joke.

"I'm going to hang up now," I said.

"I called to tell you good-bye and that I love you," he said.

I did not answer, almost hating him for putting me through this. I wished that things could have been simple like they were for Andrea and her American and British friends. I wished that Saqr would simply, truly, love me and that I could openly love him back.

"Aren't you going to say anything?" he asked.

"What should I say?"

"That you love me."

I was too frightened to answer, suddenly sure that someone else was on the line.

"Isabel, do you love me?"

I still did not answer, wishing somehow that Laila was here to tell me what to do next, that Sahaab could hear what Saqr had just said.

"Isabel, in the pink nightgown. I can imagine you right now, your green eyes, your skin, your neck..." He paused a moment, as though expecting me to stop him. When I did not say anything, he went on, slowly, deliberately.

136

I closed my eyes, envisioning this body he was describing as if it were not mine, listening as he guided me slowly down my arms, my belly, my legs. For an instant I could feel his lips on mine as though he were pressing down on me as he had in his car. I barely heard his words, now, gripping the receiver so it would not fall.

"Isabel," he said, finally, "do you love me?"

I could not help feeling that I might never get the chance to say it to him again. I wanted to say it quickly, with all the passion that was suffocating me, to show him all that I had felt for him these past two years.

Then, my hand shaking, I hung up.

LAILA

22

Isabel was spiraling into an increasingly neurotic state over that half *ajami* aristocrat.

As I watched her, I almost envied the target of the steady stream of desire I could almost see emanating from her. Hers was a classic case of ethereal love—*Antar* and *Abla, Majnun Laila*—which had me a bit apprehensive. She was too far gone for me to talk her out of it and the boy's surname alone would inhibit anyone—including myself—from telling him to leave her alone. Besides, I had no real reason to believe that his intentions toward her were not honorable.

At the same time, I had no proof that they were. From the reports that Sameer brought me and which he seemed to acquire from some mysterious network of spies, the young man was practically depraved. His father was known to drink and keep several wives, while the son was said to maintain a small menagerie of his own in London while he, supposedly, attended the university.

As my brother's sources seemed somewhat suspect, however, I did not repeat them to Isabel. Also, I knew that Sameer had recently been rather hostile toward Kuwaitis, whether part *ajami* or not. Lately, some Kuwaitis were showing an increased resentment to the growing numbers of foreigners in the country—Arab foreigners, particularly. Some weeks ago, a group of boys had threatened to have Sameer deported since he was not a native and had no legal right to stay in the country after the age of eighteen without a work permit. Such threats had become more common recently, hurled by Kuwaiti boys at their non-Kuwaiti counterparts to intimidate them whenever a fight broke out. Sameer had taken these threats personally, believing them to be typical of the attitude of Kuwaitis in general rather than that of a few, and in this frame of mind, he was apt to believe any ill rumor about them that he heard.

The other reason I did not try to dissuade Isabel from seeing Saqr was that I found myself embarking on a confusing and difficult course of my own. I could not call it passion, although in someone else's eyes it might have seemed that, for I doubted whether I could ever surrender to something so smothering. I had, as yet, never been in love, never wanted to need anyone. Not since my grandmother's death had I allowed myself to become vulnerable. Thus, this new sensation had me overwhelmed and confused.

This new path of mine began unexpectedly. One afternoon, one of Aida's visitors seemed to pay me unnecessary attention as he waited in our sitting room for her to appear. As usual, I made the coffee in the kitchen but, because Aida was still getting ready, I took it out on the tray to the guest, myself.

I could not help admiring the tall man, slim and elegant in a light gray suit, with a tiny mustache as straight as a ruler across his upper lip. He was younger than most of Aida's visitors and spoke in a soft, Egyptian accent. He seemed to be new to Kuwait—perhaps an accountant from the way he seemed to scratch numbers onto a small note pad he kept retrieving from

142

his breast pocket—having come to the desert in search of higher wages than he could get in Egypt.

It was a humid June day and I was wet with perspiration. I had pulled my hair back into a tight, unflattering ponytail since I did not care to impress any of Aida's visitors. Yet, somehow, I quickly felt awkward before this man and as I offered him the coffee and cold glass of water, I suddenly wished that I had taken the time to put on some lipstick. No sooner had he taken the cup from the tray, than I hurried back to the kitchen to escape him. But rather than finish doing my homework, I spent the next hour studying my face in the mirror as I plucked and shaped my eyebrows.

In the weeks that followed, the man, an engineer named Waleed it turned out, returned several times to our house although he never, after that first time, asked to see Aida. Instead, he would drink his cup of coffee in the sitting room and then before leaving, linger to say a few words to me if I happened to serve him the coffee or to pass by. He asked me about my school work, whether or not I planned to go on to the University after graduating from high school like many Egyptian women did. After he had gone out of his way to talk to me several times, I began to wonder whether it was I, rather than Aida, who caused him to return.

At first I was afraid that he might assume that I would join him in the back room myself! As accustomed as I was to Aida's business by now, the idea of my doing the same thing revolted me. I was so annoyed by this notion that I did something I had never done before—I told my father to tell the man never to come back to the house.

That seemed to work. We did not see Waleed for nearly a month after that. Then, one day he returned and this time my father did not object. In fact, both Aida and my father seemed to act as though this was a desirable thing. When I asked Aida why they now accepted Waleed's visits, she told me that he had told them he was lonely and simply asked to be invited over on occasion for dinner.

For some reason, this time I did not mind his coming. He was pleasant enough company to have at dinner despite his clumsy table manners—he wolfed down Aida's stews and rice as though someone were chasing him with a stick—and, strangely enough, I was no longer offended by the fact that he made no secret of his interest in me. In fact, I was rather pleased to have attracted such a man, an engineer. At first, I felt a warm flush of pleasure whenever I felt his eyes brush across my face or body, land on my fingertips when I lifted my glass to drink. Although I could not detect any sign of love for him in my own heart, I was flattered to be the source of such obvious infatuation and took to wearing tight blouses and skirts to show off my figure. I began to sense, too, that Aida was pleased with this man's staring at me. Her eyes would rest on me in a gentle, approving way then flit away before I could meet her gaze directly.

At first, I continued to worry that Aida might be wanting me to take her place, want me to encourage this man's desire enough to accompany him into a back room of the house. I was stunned. For even Aida had by now ceased to do this with all but a few selected admirers who paid handsomely, and then mostly when the rest of us were not at home. Not that we no longer needed the extra money, or that she was any less attractive than she had always been. If anything, I had seen her grow even more lovely these last few years, a subtle paleness like fresh *laban* washing over her flawless skin, the weariness in her eyes merely enhancing their beauty. She had stopped, simply, because she was tired. To her credit, she was always discreet. In all my life, she had not once talked openly about these transactions to me, not once showed me how much she had received from them nor hinted at any resentment toward my father she might have felt for his allowing her to supplement his income

144

in this way. Kuwait had not fulfilled her dreams, had not lifted us in any way from the deprivation she thought we had left behind in Lebanon. Yet, although Aida had clearly been drained of the sparkle that I had first loved in her when I still thought her to be my young cousin, she did not complain.

As grateful as I was for all her years of toil, however, I cringed at the prospect that her gentle prodding with regard to Waleed might be a hint that I should now take up where she left off. Right then I decided that I could never be happy with a man, that any man who touched me would be touching Aida so that her sad life would start all over again vicariously through me.

I soon learned, however, that Waleed's intentions were completely honorable and that he had, in fact, asked to marry me in a year when I had finished school. He had opened his life to my father, told him of his family's modest background in Cairo as well as told him his present earnings which he assured him would increase since chemical engineers were much in demand in Kuwait. My parents, thus, were now in the process of observing him to see whether or not he would make a suitable husband.

My father had, of course, enthusiastically relayed Waleed's proposal to Aida who in turn informed me. I could tell that in Aida's and my father's eyes, it finally looked as though everything would turn out all right, after all. By my marrying well, one burden was about to be lifted from their lives and their luck might change. Perhaps this desirable marriage would wash away the excruciating remnants of pain of both Bilal's and my grandmother's deaths which had never ceased to haunt us all. It had always seemed as if their deaths had been a punishment of some sort for our having left Lebanon. By their daughter securing a good future in Kuwait, their ten years of suffering in the desert would finally seem justified.

However, nothing for my family was ever simple and this episode with Waleed proved to be merely a distraction from the other, unforeseen, road that I was destined to travel. For

the course that I was to embark on, although perhaps insti-
gated by this man's interest in me, was a much more treacher-
ous one that I neither asked for nor could prevent.

One night, after the third or fourth of these dinners with
Waleed which I found myself growing accustomed to, though I
was sometimes annoyed by his persistent doting, I lay in my bed
wondering what would come of it. I was nearly seventeen and
had one more year of school. I wanted to be someone, to go on
to the university as Isabel and I planned, to find a good job so
that I would never have to depend on anyone—certainly not a
man—to provide me with a good living, and here I was already
considering a marriage prospect.

Waleed was, obviously, well off enough that neither Aida nor
my father objected to his presence at our table where he seemed
to feast on me as much as on the food. The only one who
seemed bothered, to my surprise, was Sameer. His eyes would
ignite with what seemed like a sense of powerlessness that he
must have felt each time a man had come for Aida. Several
times, in fact, he came to my defense by gruffly telling me to go
and make the coffee just as Waleed's gaze grew unbearable.

What came to follow between my brother and me was, although at first inexplicable to both of us, a thing which gradually began to fill a mutual craving for comfort and love that my
mother and father had somehow denied us.

It began simply. I saw, only later, that it had been inevitable.

One night after dinner, my door slowly creaked open. It was
March and the open window drew in enough moonlight along
with the cool breeze for me to recognize the slight stoop of his
neck, the high ridge of his nose. It happened quickly, without
warning. Suddenly, all I knew was that I was drawing back my
sheets for him, closing out the rest of the house and the world
in that instant.

"Laila," came his voice, a sob. At first, I could not answer.

"Say that you don't love him," Sameer said, his voice steadier
now, stronger, as he lay beside me.

146

"Of course I don't love him."

"You won't marry him and leave."

I touched his course, coiled hair lightly as he lay his face on the pillow.

"Say you won't—" he persisted, his voice muffled.

"I won't."

"You know I love you," he said, sobbing again.

I felt faint with terror. Inside me welled an emptiness that I had never known before. "I know," I whispered.

For the first time, I encountered a loneliness as voluminous and blinding as my own, a yearning as strong as my own. We were children, again, meeting each other for the first time, told that we were brother and sister, resenting each other yet knowing that we had to be allies in the desperate, strange world that Aida and our father had carved out for us.

So it was, as though it were the most natural thing in the world, that I welcomed my brother Sameer into my arms.

ISABEL

23

Death was something that began to preoccupy me a great deal in high school. Perhaps it was the realization that I was growing up that led me to dwell on the inevitable eventuality of death.

I had never seen a cemetery in Kuwait. I had not seen stone markers nor plots of land set aside for that purpose. Neither had I ever been to a funeral although I knew that the dead were washed and wrapped in white cloth and then buried before sundown. The Kuwaitis seemed to make little fuss over death and the mourning period was short, as though it were shameful to belabor something that was intended to be an inevitable part of nature. I had the vague feeling that when people died, here, they simply dissolved back into the sand.

I was reminded of death frequently enough, however, because of the burnings that took place behind our school in Fahaheel where there was a Hindu crematorium for the Indian workers to burn their dead. On any afternoon, from our second floor classrooms, we would suddenly see curls of smoke from the plot of land adjacent to our school and know that there had been a death among the Hindus. There was something uniquely peaceful about these scenes at which the men who had brought the corpse to the pyre would calmly watch the fire crackle brilliantly and finally smolder until they put it out. Despite the revulsion exhibited by most of the girls and teachers who found the idea of cremation particularly distasteful, what struck me most about these episodes was how sad it was that these people died so far from their homes in India.

One spring afternoon, I rode my bicycle to the stables to take Noor out for a ride. There was an immense stillness over the compound, the sun hanging heavy and low beyond the refinery as the day mellowed into a halo of warmth.

Some of the expatriates had started to keep barnyard animals—lambs, rabbits, pigeons, and chickens—at the stables, housing them in wired-off sections of the large, wooden freight crates left from the overseas shipments. An annoying clucking, cooing and bleating now invaded the former calm of the stables as the animals thrived and multiplied despite the heat and the occasional barbecues when they disappeared from the crates to be slaughtered and roasted.

The horses were in their stalls feeding. Conspicuously absent was *Wadha*, the new filly that for the past two months had entertained me by galloping around the corral as she raced with her shadow. Like Noor in her younger days, Wadha had been hard to restrain. She was the same deep red as my small Hidiya used to be and she had a white star on her forehead. She was so beautiful that I had asked my father several times about the possibility of buying her from her owner. We could use another horse, I kept telling him, for ever since Hidiya had died, whenever we rode together my father had let me ride Noor and had borrowed someone else's horse for himself.

152

Then, early one morning, when the stable boy had gone to feed the horses, he had found Wadha hanging limply from the fence by her red main which had caught in the barbed wire running along the top. Her memory saddened me every time I entered the stables, now, for even if I were never to own her, myself, I would have been content just to watch her frisky prancing.

I saddled Noor, but instead of heading for the beach, I rode toward the refinery and through the gate of the barbed wire fence that surrounded our compound, past the guard at the check-post, feeling a rush of exaltation at being free. Then, I urged Noor into a reckless gallop.

The powdery sand below her hoofs flew ahead of us toward a mauve horizon, as smooth as if it had just been swept with a soft, feather broom. We were on raw, virgin ground, now. Except for the occasional lizard or snake hole and the three-pronged prints of birds, there was no sign that anything else had trampled the sand before us. Tufts of ecru-colored camel grass sprouted above each small mound of sand, the tiny hills that made up the desert. The terrain was like that of some deserted planet in outer space. It was hard to imagine that this solitary place was even inhabited, although the refinery's ever-burning orange flare in the distance was a constant reminder of the compound and the hundreds employed there.

Unlike the villages closer to Kuwait city, the desert surrounding our compound had not changed much in the ten years that we had been here. Except for the new telephone poles and wires along the tar road, it was still an oasis of open spaces with only occasional black or brown bedouin tents between the compound and the next towns of Shuaiba, Fahaheel and Ahmadi. I was happy to have grown up with this natural landscape as a playground—the sand and lucid waters of the sea, a single ancient crab-apple tree near the stables to climb, spring dandelions that we held under one another's chins to see whether or not we liked butter. Once, Andrea and I had discovered a bedouin woman who had just given birth in the desert while tending her goats. She had sent us off to the guard at the compound gate to get her a drink of water, and had become upset when the guard had radioed the compound clinic for an ambulance to fetch her and her infant to the clinic to be checked by the doctor. It was a life that was very different from those who lived in the city of Kuwait, itself, and I knew that it would not last much longer.

I reached the main road. An occasional car thundered by, scattering pebbles and sand, rattling over the holes in the tar-surfaced road. Then all was quiet again with only a whispering breeze rifling the sand. To the right, the road led to Shuaiba and Fahaheel; to the left were the oil fields, the small border town of Khafje, then Saudi Arabia. The Tower of Dreams lay in that direction.

Though tempted to turn left toward the Tower, I turned right. I knew that Saqr was not there, but also because I did not want to anchor the Tower to reality by seeing it from this perspective. From the sea it was a miracle. The sweep of sandstone walls, the sunken windows, the sea gulls perched on the square wind towers were so entrenched in my mind from those first times that I saw it that each time I ventured there I worried that something had been changed, been rebuilt or renovated, destroying that first image.

So, I rode further into the desert, away from the sea. Then, for no particular reason, I began to think of Laila.

We had been so close as children and yet, now, we seemed to be splitting off, like branches of a tree growing in opposite directions, each searching out its own light. Although we still spent a good part of the day in school together, it seemed as though once we had entered puberty, we had somehow reverted back to the different influences of our families. I had

154

remained an only child while Laila had a brother. Also, Laila's Arab mother seemed to be more of a sister to her than mine could ever be to me, seeming to confide in her rather than be a parent to her.

I remembered when we were thirteen and had begun to experiment with make-up and removing the hair on our legs and from under our arms. Like my mother, I had used a razor for this purpose. The image of my mother taking a bath, stroking her leg with her gold razor, was one of my earliest memories and I was certain that I would do this myself. The first times I used her razor, however, I cut myself mercilessly. Probably not wishing to embarrass me, she had not said anything, though it must have been obvious to her that her razor dulled twice as fast and that my legs glowed like mirrors. For Laila, removing her hair was a much more elaborate ritual. Instead of a razor, her mother boiled up a sticky taffy of sugar, water, and lemon which she manipulated over Laila's legs until all the hairs were pulled out. The fact that this hurt did not deter Laila, who was determined to be a smooth as I.

We had also had our first menstrual periods within months of each other. My mother had presented me with a box of sanitary pads and a cup of hot water laced with a few drops of whiskey to soothe my aches. Laila's mother had given her cotton soaked in rubbing alcohol to put on her stomach for the pain, but instead of disposable pads, Laila used white cloths which her mother washed nightly. When I had first learned this, I thought it disgusting to share something so private with anyone else, even with one's own mother. I was glad for my modern mother to whom I would never give my blood-soaked cloths to wash nor my legs to shave. Nor could I imagine her wanting to do such a thing. It was not without a pang of envy, however, that I thought of this intimate exchange between Laila and her mother for it was something I was not likely to ever have with my own.

Wondering what it must be like to share such a cocoon of

155

closeness with one's mother so absorbed me as I rode further away from the compound that I nearly passed the low mounds that suddenly appeared on my right.

I pulled in my reins. In a clearing, were several peculiar elevations topped with a scattering of stones. I had never seen such mounds before. Guiding Noor through them, careful to avoid her stepping on them since I had the distinct feeling that the mounds were graves, I counted five of them. Four could pass for natural elevations except that they were all oblong, free of any camel grass and were all pointed in the same direction. The fifth was noticeably askew, its stones heaped up carelessly as though it had been an afterthought.

I dismounted, holding the reins securely lest Noor bolt off and leave me standing amidst the mounds. The stones had obviously been painstakingly gathered from the sandy desert and placed over each mound to mark it or perhaps to guard it from any roving dogs or goats. There was no other sign that anyone had been there, and no indication of what, if anything, lay below the mounds.

Then, something small sparkled on the ground near one of the mounds. I bent and picked it up. It was a gold ring, a spiral snake with a small, ruby eye. It looked somewhat familiar and I rubbed it against my trousers to clean it, wondering where I had seen it before.

Suddenly, I felt a stab in my chest. In a flash, I was back on Noor, urging her toward the compound, my mind racing.

The ring belonged to Laila! I was sure of it. She wore it on her middle finger. Laila had not been in school for several days, supposedly at home with a cold. My hands trembled. I did not even dare to think what finding Laila's ring near some freshly dug graves meant. I only knew to hold tightly to the reigns and barely saw the ground beneath Noor's hoofs as she raced back in the direction of the black plumes of smoke from the refinery.

Nobody answered the telephone in Laila's house when I rang. This calmed me somewhat. I assumed that she and her family had gone out. It was absurd to think that anything had happened to her simply because I had found her ring in the desert.

Yet, I hardly slept that night. I kicked off my blankets and then, freezing from the cool air-conditioner, pulled them up to my chin again. My thoughts were a crazed jumble, egged on by the pelting sounds of dripping water from the air conditioner outside my window. I saw Laila's face, obstinate, beautiful. Next to my parents', hers was the oldest and dearest face of my childhood.

In a dream I saw Sahaab, her round, smiling face eternally childlike, telling me again that Laila's end would not be a good one. I saw Sahaab as she was in a picture I had taken of her last year when she had insisted on being photographed beside my horse. I had taken the picture, and I had tried to get her to move closer to the horse, secretly hoping that Noor would nudge her flat onto her face. In the dream, I saw Sahaab's blind father, too, heaving himself up those endless steps to the top of the mosque's minaret, his cane tapping out a rhythm as it guided him on his climb.

Toward morning, I sank into a more familiar dream of being a child again, playing cards in the afternoons in Laila's little courtyard, her mother fixing rice and green beans for us, smiling at us as she sat nearby in a glimmering dress.

"You promise you won't tell anyone?" Laila said the next morning as she slipped the ring back onto her middle finger. To my relief, she was very much alive despite my fitful night.

"You know I never do," I said, not wanting her to suspect how much I had feared for her.

"Sameer is teaching me to drive. That's why we were out there where there isn't much traffic."

157

"Sameer is teaching you to drive?" I was as jealous as I was amazed. I had always thought that I would be the one to learn to drive first because on several occasions my father had taken me to the empty parking lot near the beach and taught me to shift gears and drive in wide circles. However, my father had had little time lately to repeat these endeavors.

"It's wonderful," said Laila, her eyes half closing in a swoon as she held out her hands in front of her as though she were clutching a steering wheel. "And the best part is that he promises to buy me my own car when I'm seventeen. An MG."

"Sameer is going to buy you a car?" I was even more surprised—Sameer had never done a thing for his sister.

"Next year," she said, closing her eyes completely. "Next year you and I will be as free as birds."

"Free as birds." I echoed her happy sounds now that she had included me in her wild plans. For a moment, I shared this scenario with her and it did sound good. I imagined myself driving to visit Saqr whenever I chose, going shopping with Laila in the city for new clothes, visiting our friends whenever we wanted...and all in a red MG!

"You still could have stopped by to see me since you were so close," I said.

"I wanted to, but Sameer is a bit shy."

"Of me?"

"He doesn't know your family," she said.

Yet I knew that the reason that she had not come over had less to do with Sameer being shy of my parents than with the fact that she had simply, not thought to. Laila could be quite self-absorbed and she had doubtlessly been so mesmerized by her driving and the prospect of getting her own car that she had not thought of me or anyone else that afternoon.

24

I arrived home from school and threw myself onto my bed, screaming as though in the throws of one of my old childhood temper tantrums. I yelled in outrage, for whenever I stopped, the hollow pain cut into me and twisted my stomach with nausea.

The night before, I had seen Andrea at the club after a movie. It had been her last night in Kuwait before she returned to London to start school the next day. As usual, she asked me about Saqr and, as usual, I told her that I had not seen him. Then, she told me that she had heard that he had a new girlfriend.

"I'm sure he has several in London," I said, casually, feigning indifference.

But she had persisted. "It's somebody here. A local girl."

It had taken me an entire night and morning to get over my numbness.

"Isabel, what on earth is the matter with you?" my mother

called, from the hall outside my locked door.

"Nothing," I cried.

"Then stop all that screaming."

I licked the tears streaming down to my lips, sucking the salt from the strands of hair stuck to my cheeks. I started to sob again.

There was a soft knock at my bedroom door.

"What?"

"Isabel, open the door."

I did not move.

"Come on, silly," she coaxed. "Please."

It was her old playfulness, her strength in rising above pettiness or unhappiness that I heard through the wall. Just as she had smiled when the veiled, *abayaed* woman had reached through the airplane seats to touch my hair on our very first trip to Kuwait, just as she had listened, with amusement, to my fretting about the overwhelming prospect of returning to the Shuaiba school where nobody spoke English, her voice now seemed to penetrate fear and sadness with the stoic solidity of iron. Perhaps it was the memory of our closeness on those afternoons when I had lain next to her in bed listening to one of her made-up stories that made me open my bedroom door now and thrust myself into her arms.

She stroked my hair as we sat on the bed, holding my hand in hers which was always whiter and softer than mine despite her hours of gardening. I hinted with various grunts and nods in response to her probing that I was experiencing boy trouble.

"I wish I could make it easier for you," she said.

"Why does it have to hurt so much?" I asked, angrily.

"I don't know," she said, looking genuinely bewildered.

"Did you ever feel this way?"

"I did."

"With Daddy?"

She lifted one of her softly-penciled eyebrows. "I was more sensible by the time I met him."

160

"With who, then?"

"I forgot," she said, looking right past me for a moment into some vision of her own, before smiling with what I thought was sad reassurance. "But you *do* get over it."

She rose and squeezed my hand and I tried to squeeze her back, if only to indicate that she had helped me. Yet rather than feel comforted, I felt cheated. I was surprised and angry. It had somehow not occurred to me before that there would be some sorrows in my life that not even my mother could chase away!

Stretched out on my bed after she left, I gazed for a long time at the short, yellow curtains at my windows that she had made for me some years ago. For the first time I noticed that they had become flimsy and frayed from the sun beating on them all day. They were worn so thin that when I reached up and tugged at them now they tore without the slightest effort, their fibers disintegrating in my fingers like sand. Just as my heart was now disintegrating.

A local girl. Andrea's crisp, British syllables reverberated in an intruding chorus. Why did she have to be so cruel? She probably meant a Kuwaiti girl. It was inevitable, of course. Laila had warned me that he would never be permitted to love a foreigner.

I began to think that we had lived in the desert too long, that we had become trapped in an abysmal existence in a place that we could never, truly, be a part of. Perhaps had we lived in some place where there were green forests, where there were rivers and fields, we would be different, not so worn through, not hurting, aching, and shredding apart so much.

I began to see the desert as doing strange things to those of us who did not belong there. Laila, Sahaab, myself, even our parents—we were not the people in Kuwait that we might have been elsewhere.

I rubbed my face against the pillowcase, my breaths hot and muffled against the sheets. I thought of my mother, stretched

161

out in bed in the afternoons reading and napping, passing away the endless hours and years of the harsh, desert life.

Late November saw the desert at its best. It was cool and dry and promised a pleasant winter. We had started our last year of school and we seemed to all be surging with a certain sweet giddiness at having to face the unknown, soon. It was mostly a feeling of exhilaration that welled up inside me at the prospect of parting with my childhood. Rather than sadden me, this feeling seemed to infuse me with added energy needed for the endless school work and examinations required for graduation. Yet, as though unaware of the optimism all around us, Laila suddenly started to behave strangely.

It began slowly. At first, I noticed only that she avoided my eyes whenever I spoke to her. Then, she began to disappear during break or lunchtime which we usually spent together, leading me to wonder whether she was upset with me for some reason. When I asked her what was wrong, her face seemed to close and take on a mask of superiority, an expression that I was accustomed to by now as a defense she used whenever there was something she was not able or did not want to discuss.

About that same time, my neighbor Andrea returned from London for the winter holidays. As usual, she telephoned me. This time, it was I who inquired whether she had heard anything about Saqr. She told me that she had heard that he was already back although she had not seen him at any of the parties she had been to.

A year had passed since my afternoon with him in his car. It was a strange and sometimes painful year yet one in which I felt that I had taken ten strides forward for every one that the other girls in my school, including Laila, had taken. The main reason for this was that all the unfulfilled longing for Saqr had pushed me to seek refuge in books.

162

With my mother's help, I had selected some English classics—Thackery and D.H. Lawrence. In addition, on one of her trips back to Kuwait from London, Andrea had brought me a list and several books that students in England were reading: Sartre, Simone de Beauvoir, Gunther Grass. Through these writers, I felt myself being slowly awakened to Western ideas and was surprised to feel this new knowledge seeping into me like a long lost child who had suddenly been found and brought home. I began to sense I was entering a new sphere, one as yet unknown to my Arab friends, and at times I felt quite superior in my newly expanded vision.

Yet, despite all this growth on the one hand, when I heard that Saqr was back, it was as though all this new confidence and strength had been washed out of me. I felt as though I had been abruptly thrown back into first grade in the hot, humid room of the Shuaiba school where nobody understood a word I said. I suddenly felt joy and sadness with an intensity I had never known—blushing the moment his name was mentioned and feeling almost ill with the fear that I would not see him the next. Indeed, it seemed as if all the reading in the world would not enable me to understand and control the absurd, relentless passion I felt for Saqr. I hated myself for being so vulnerable, for squirming at the very thought of seeing him, at the memory of his strong, confident arms around me.

During study hall in school the next day, I told Laila that Saqr was back, both to share the burden of my feelings with someone but, also, hoping to spark in her some of the old enthusiasm she had shown in my love life.

All she said at this revelation, however, was "Have you memorized Al Mutanabi yet?"

I stared at her, not comprehending. Then I remembered. Al Mutanabi was a poet whose work we needed to have memorized for the exam in two weeks. In my excitement over Saqr I had almost forgotten.

"Have you?" I asked.

"I'm almost through," she said, going back to copying a page of poetry into her notebook.

"I thought you'd be interested," I said.

"In what?" she said, without looking at me.

"In Saqr's being here. He'll probably call me."

She still did not look at me. "Since when are you more interested in school work than in romance?" I said, joking, hurt that something so crushing to me failed to touch her.

"Will you see him this time?" she said, finally, with a sigh.

"If he calls."

"And if he doesn't?"

"Then, I suppose I won't."

I realized that I had not thought of the possibility that Saqr would not call me. I had rehearsed the scenario that would take place between us so well that the thought that he might not contact me had not even occurred to me.

"Well, it's not much of a romance if you don't see him, is it?" Laila said, still copying.

Her hair had completely slid over the side of her face turned toward me. It was an opaque veil—black, enveloping, bewitching.

Now that she had put the possibility of Saqr's not calling me into my head, I was obsessed with it.

"Don't you think he'll call?" I asked.

She continued to write.

"Tell me what to do," I begged.

"About what?"

"What if he doesn't call? Should I try to contact him? What will he think?"

She put down her fountain pen and pushed back her hair as though it were some heavy load she had to shed, and asked, wearily, "Do you care what he thinks?"

Her face was pale, as though all the copying into the notebook had drained the blood from her body.

"Of course I care," I said.

164

"Then, don't call."

There was a sudden commotion at the front of the room where several girls were throwing something back and forth. This seemed to absorb Laila, as if she had momentarily forgotten me.

"So, I should call him?"

Laila lowered her glance back to my face. It seemed to take an immense effort for her to refocus on me, but when she did, her eyes were moist and uncommonly tender.

"Go to him while you can, Isabel," she said, picking up her pen.

Though her voice had a certain urgency, as though she actually cared about whatever became of me and Saqr, at that moment I felt as empty and cold as if she had stood and walked away.

I thought, then, that I had lost her forever.

Despite my worrying about Saqr and my impatient waiting for his call, it was Laila's sudden moodiness, which I could not help attributing to something I must have done, that distracted me. For several days I did nothing after school but listen to my old records and rummage through a box filled with old school treasures: scraps of embroidery done in the second grade, an old wooden ruler with an ink heart drawn on it with Laila's and my initials, a collection of torn papers—secret notes passed during class—which I had preserved. Among those, I was surprised to find Laila's frayed, scribbled note from the bus driver.

Finally, one afternoon the call came.

"Isabel?"

I recognized Saqr's voice. It was as though I had been waiting for this moment all my life, as though I knew it even before he spoke, from his breath, the way he always hesitated before uttering the first word, in case it was not me who had picked up the receiver.

"Isabel?"

All my unhappiness evaporated. "You're back?" I asked, knowing that he had been back at least ten days.

Until now, I had been upset that he had not called, worried that he had forgotten me. The vision of the 'local girl' that Andrea had mentioned months ago had loomed like a hideous monster in my mind. Yet the unexpected sound of his voice this afternoon soothed the anger and fear out of my consciousness.

"I miss you," he said.

"I miss you, too," I said, hugging the receiver to my ear. I was spinning, sinking deeper and deeper.

"I want to see you."

"I do, too," I heard myself say, wanting to touch him through the telephone wire.

"When?"

"When?" I repeated, unable to think, wanting to tell him everything, afraid to tell him anything. "I'm not sure."

"I'll come to your school," he said.

"No!"

I remembered the teasing that I had endured from some of the girls at school following his last visit. It had taken a year for some of them to forget about it.

"Where, then?"

"Maybe we had better not."

"But I want to see you."

"Why haven't you called before?"

There was silence at the other end, as though I had spoken into a great void.

"Isabel," he said, his voice searching, soft, "come to my place on the beach. Come to the Tower."

"No."

"Why? No one will be there."

"I can't."

"At least meet me halfway. Between your place and the Tower. Can you get there?"

It sounded daring, but somehow not as outrageous as my going all the way to the Tower. "I can come on my horse," I said, trembling.

"Good. I'll meet you there."

"When?"

"At six o'clock tomorrow evening," he said.

I did not answer. All at once I felt terrified at the prospect of being found out and, even more, of actually seeing him after so long.

"Isabel?"

"Yes?"

"You'll be there?"

I forced myself to wait, to sound almost reluctant. Finally, I said, "Yes."

I listened into the phone long after he had hung up, wanting there to be something more. Then I replaced the receiver and lay on the bed and cried as I had done when I had heard of the 'local girl'. But this time I cried with unfathomable relief.

LAILA

25

It was *Eid al Fitr*, the three-day holiday after the month of fasting. *Ramadhan* had seemed to fly by this year. It had been easy to do without food and water all day when the weather was cool and the days short. Coming two weeks early each year, *Ramadhan* would fall in Autumn two more times before we would have to start fasting in the summer. I usually enjoyed fasting, anyway, enjoyed even the pangs of hunger because they reminded me of the elaborate meal Aida would be home preparing for the evening breakfast and especially the thought of the syrup-drenched *qataif* pancakes that she filled with walnuts or sweet cheese and fried fresh each night during this month. As much as the variety of foods which filled our table during these evening breakfasts, I relished the gaiety in the streets each evening after the sundown meal when my parents and I would stroll through the festively-lit streets of Shuaiba or Fahaheel until midnight. We would buy useless trinkets, or even small pieces of jewelry, ice-cream , *Ramadhan* cookies, and fried Indian *samosas* filled with potatoes and chilies. Everyone seemed happier after a day of fasting, more generous, too. Even when Aida roused us from sleep for our last meal before dawn, there would be a jovial mood around the kitchen table as we ate bread, cheese, and fruit to fortify ourselves for the following day. Even my father would tell a few jokes before going back to bed.

This Eid day, my father took Aida and me for a ride through Kuwait city, to see all the new construction that had taken place the past year. No longer the quiet, desert town we had seen when we first arrived and which, even now, I remembered so vividly, Kuwait had suddenly filled with buildings of six or more stories, the concrete structures sprawling into the desert like a slumbering army of locusts for as far as the eye could sea. Only a few areas seemed familiar from years ago when we drove past the Ruler's stately long-windowed residence at *Sha'ab* on the sea, and the government offices in *Dasman* palace closer in town. Children ran through the streets in their new clothes, girls in colorful taffeta dresses, the little boys in new suits, many of them clutching the new toys they had received. Some children carried sparklers that ignited the air before them. One man walked down an alleyway carrying a small, live lamb to be butchered for the evening feast. It was the knowledge that we could eat any time we wanted to, a forgotten luxury during the past month, that contributed to this general feeling of intoxicating elation. It was easy to lose oneself in the merriment, if only for a few hours.

My grandmother could have predicted it—with a death there would also be a birth.

After Sameer began coming to my room at night, I felt a slow degeneration—like a tree being stripped of its bark or a flower of its petals so that all that remained was a limp, weakened core. We clung to each other through a deep privation and a love too perverse to be admitted which seemed to rob me of any ambition or will to keep up with my old life, my studies, or my friends. For I suddenly found the companions of my difficult childhood, including Isabel, all deathly boring. Yet, all the time it was I, not they, who was slowly dying.

Of course I knew that what Sameer and I did was wrong, just as he knew it was, but neither of us could face up to this admission. Sameer, already nineteen, must have had some earlier physical experience with women for he had occasionally mumbled about prostitutes in telephone conversations with his friends. But he never talked about them, or about any of the girls that he met when he went out with his friends, with me. He seemed to have some fierce desire to exert his power over women while at the same time harboring some visceral dread of them. Perhaps it was simply a need to get back at our mother for abandoning him and his father for other men. For Sameer never seemed to understand Aida's role in supporting our family, did not seem to appreciate that on our father's income, alone, we could never have afforded even the few luxuries we were able to have as children such as a television and car. Perhaps, too, he was less able than I to ignore the looks slapped on us by some of the neighbor women, although I doubt that any of them knew for certain of Aida's activities. Whatever his reasons, Sameer carried a boundless burden of anger for Aida which he never tired of finding some new way to express. This, I think, he believed he had supremely accomplished through dominating me.

For my part, why did I allow him this satisfaction when I could have easily chosen marriage to Waleed and a life of respectability as the wife of an engineer as my parents were hoping? Along with the fact that I had not been able to bring myself to love Waleed these past months, despite his obvious devotion to me, the vision of a future with him paled in the face of my sudden, overwhelming need to comfort and nurture my brother where our mother had so miserably failed. I felt sorry for Sameer. At the same time, I felt safe with him. If nothing else, we could cry together as we had that night so long ago after Bilal's death. Somehow, we trusted each other. We shared a shocking secret about our mother, after all, as well as the secret about my own birth out of wedlock. Perhaps we believed that together we could manage to escape, to go back to Lebanon, to start a new life away from our father and Aida and the desert that had bred shame in us rather than give us the good life that we had been promised.

What Sameer did promise me, now, was a car. He had started a job with an air-conditioner maintenance firm and was paid well. Whenever I hinted that I did not want him to come back to my bedroom, he would tell me of the multitude of things that were possible if we stayed together, the places we could go, the things we could buy with the money he earned from his new job. The first thing was a car, he insisted, a red one, an MG that would make me the envy of all of my friends. He was already teaching me how to drive our father's car.

I told him that I wanted to help him pay for it, that I could sew or tutor elementary students for money. This, however, did not seem to impress him. Instead he came up with the idea of photographing me and selling the pictures. Pictures of pretty girls would sell like water to the lonely men living in a desert without wives and families, he told me. "You have to be creative to make money," he explained.

I was shocked by his suggestion. The last few months I had refused to think of him as using me. Now, I was angry that he was actually contemplating it. I knew that the money would benefit us both, but I also felt that it was I, alone, who would be sacrificing for something he alleged was a gift to me. I thought I detected in this idea of photographing me a selfish need on Sameer's part to recreate me, to reinvent me through the camera into something that better fit his fancy, perhaps into a complete flesh and blood sister as I should have been all along

174

rather than his mother's child from some mysterious phantom who had lurked in our midst all these years. But Sameer was not one to look into himself for answers to anything and he was already smitten by his idea of making money off photographing me, as if it were the brainchild of the century.

Then, later in November, something happened that threatened to destroy our plans. I stopped menstruating.

My uniform grew tight, my arms and breasts grew fuller, and Aida's jasmine cologne, usually pleasingly fresh, sent me heaving over the toilet. After several bouts of this nausea it occurred to me what was happening. My stomach sank with fear when I realized what was growing there.

I knew I had to tell Sameer. After all, this was all his fault. His child!

Yet, I had come to know my brother's thinking all too well these past few months, and I knew that telling him was not a good idea. He would be as seized with panic as I was. He would say that a child would change everything, would force us to leave home earlier than planned—just when he was starting to save money. At this point, his caring for my welfare would pale beside his ambition to leave.

I grew distraught thinking that he might get angry enough to hit me the way he used to when we were children even though I sensed that he had grown fond of me, almost dependent on me, in planning our mutual escape. I decided not to tell him, sure that everything would work out for us if I remained calm. So, instead, I told him that it would be a good time to start selling my pictures. He agreed, and bought film for his camera.

The pictures he took of me that day showed a serene, round, moon-like face and a soft, supple body appropriately unfocused and mysterious. Yet, I had to wonder whether anyone would actually buy them since I was sure my face spelled pregnancy to anyone who looked hard enough.

175

I began, almost immediately, to have a mysterious telepathy with my unborn child whom I already thought of, inadvertently, as my nephew or niece. I was sure that the child was unhappy. In a dream one night, the baby looked exactly like Bilal as I remembered him best—with rose-white skin, dancing, black eyes, and legs as soft as freshly baked bread. In the dream, I stared at my child, content to gaze at Bilal's beloved and missed face once more, remembering the way that his soft, black curls had floated about his head as he took his first, faltering steps. When I went closer to him, I discovered a small, black object on his belly. It was a scorpion! My heart seemed to stop beating in the instant that I grabbed the thing with my bare hands and hurled it against the wall just as I woke up, hot and writhing from the sharp pains in my own abdomen, exactly where the scorpion had been on my child in the dream.

But, I was no longer dreaming. I shook with the pain that tugged at my insides as if a fire were broiling me from within. It was several hours later that the child must have left my body, swam out of me in the torrent of blood and guilt, ending its short existence.

I did not go to school the next day. I rolled up the bloodied sheet with the small clumps that I knew had been my child, and hid it underneath my bed. I no longer felt the nausea shaking me when I stood up, but the need to tell someone, anyone, was choking me. Yet I could not tell my family. Not even my closest friend, Isabel, could possibly understand something like this. Angelic Isabel. How would she regard me if I burdened her with such horror?

In the afternoon, Aida came into my room with a cup of hot, boiled mint leaves. "I could have given my daughter something besides my cramps," she said with a guilty smile, assuming that I was simply having my monthly. Her own pains often sent her to bed with stomach and back spasms and she must have thought

176

that I had inherited this predisposition. In truth, however, I hardly felt a thing any more during these times.

"I'll be all right," I said, taking the hot cup from her.

She tried to sit on the edge of the bed. When I made no movement to make room for her, she gently lifted my legs and placed my feet on her lap. It had been years since she had sat beside me in bed and it was hard not to give in and confess everything to her as her cool hands rubbed my toes.

It was too late for this, however. Somehow, had Sameer and I been fully connected none of this would have happened. I forced my face to remain impassive and sipped the hot drink in silence.

I lay awake all night with the single thought that the bloody mass that was my child was still wrapped up in the sheet beneath my bed. Somehow, though I was not particularly religious, I was upset by the thought that its small soul would never swim in the rivers of heaven nor see the faces of the angels.

The next morning, as I stood at our door in my nightgown and watched my friends rush past me down the sunny alleyway to catch the bus to school, I slipped a note to one of the girls to deliver to Sahaab.

The idea had occurred to me just at dawn, when the hours of sleeplessness must have sharpened my brain, that I must bury my child. I had to do it properly, and I needed help. The best help, under the circumstances, was someone with knowledge of holy matters. It had to be Sahaab, the *mu'athin's* daughter.

I was surprised when I saw Sahaab actually waiting by the side of the road at the designated spot, nearly a kilometer beyond the compound where she and Isabel lived. I had picked it because she could walk there and it was not too far a ride for me by taxi. I paid the driver and got out, telling him to return in an hour, ignoring his curiosity at my wanting to be let off in the middle of the desert.

Sahaab could not have appeared more delighted at this clandestine meeting. She waved enthusiastically from the side of the black road, nearly enshrouded in dust from the taxi which had swerved into the sand and started back in the direction from which I had come.

"Have you been sick?" she yelled, running up to me, her mouth in that wide, stupid grin.

Normally I paid Sahaab as little attention as possible and often wondered how Isabel could stand listening to her brainless chatter to and from school each day.

"You didn't tell anyone, did you?" I said, sternly.

"Oh, no," she said, her eyes wide, her face collapsing as if I had accused her instead of merely asked her. But I had no time to worry about whether or not she was telling the truth. Obviously, she wanted to be the object of my undying trust and was practically lusting after my reasons for summoning her.

"Listen, Sahaab," I began, hearing my own words tumbling out of my mouth like dice. "Something terrible has happened and I'm entrusting you with the biggest secret you'll ever have to keep."

I told her quickly and simply that my mother had gotten pregnant and had aborted. Because my mother was too ill to get out of bed, she had entrusted me to burying what would have been my baby sister or brother. Naturally, neither my father nor brother knew anything of this and she, Sahaab, was not even to think about it after we completed our business that afternoon.

I had asked for her help, I told her, because she surely knew of such matters since her father was the *mu'athin*. When I added that not even Isabel knew of this, her eyes seemed to melt with pleasure at being my sole confidant.

"I promised Mother that I would give it a proper burial," I said, scanning the level dunes before us for some large clump of camel grass or ridge that would shield the grave from view. The sprouts of grass were too small to hide anything and most of the plain was flat and as smooth as silk. I trudged further into the desert and Sahaab followed me, mute. Finally, I settled on a spot some way off the road that looked right. It looked windswept and calm. "This is it," I said.

"It will have to face Mecca. My father prays this way," she said, determining which was east from where we stood.

Together, we knelt and scraped at the parched, hard desert until we had a hole big enough to bury a cat.

"Turn away now," I instructed her.

She did so, reluctantly, while I retrieved the knotted sheet, placed it in the earth, and immediately scooped fistfuls of sand over it. Sahaab turned back in time to see the last bit of muslin with pink embroidery vanish.

As if on cue, we began whispering the *fatiha* as we continued to build up our mound. The prayer soothed me. The child would, finally, be admitted to heaven. Sameer and I would be forgiven.

"*Thoraya*," I said, suddenly.

"What?" asked Sahaab, brushing sand off her large hands.

"It needs a name. I always wanted a sister named Thoraya. It was my grandmother's name."

"It could have been a boy," Sahaab said.

"I'm sure it was a girl," I said, lifting my head. My neck ached, and I felt a heaviness settle around us like the blanket of gray clouds that were slowly arranging and rearranging themselves overhead as though it might rain.

"We had better cover it with stones to keep the sand in place," Sahaab said.

I stood and imitated her, feeling weak from loss of blood and sleep the night before, gathering what pebbles I could see through the tears glazing my eyes. We placed them over the tidy, little mound.

It was all over.

Yet, the memory of last night, of the clot of blood that had been beating in me these last three months and that now lay in

179

the sheet made me ill. I wanted to go home.

Sahaab, though, seemed oddly rejuvenated. "We must make more mounds to fool anyone who might want to dig this up," she said, with sudden authority.

I watched her determined brow move with intensity as she dug. Beneath the beads of perspiration circling her face was a fierce glow.

"It's not necessary," I said, wiping my eyes from the tears and dust, wanting to get away from the place at once. "In a few days the sand will have shifted and it won't be noticeable any more."

"We can't take that chance."

I stood watching as she knelt a little distance from the grave and formed a new mound. She practically embraced the earth, using her arms and elbows to gather as much sand as possible, shaping it like the first grave but pointing it in a different direction. Her frantic motions, like some mad woman performing an act comprehensible only to herself, made me cringe.

"I don't have time. The taxi will be coming for me any minute," I said, impatient.

"You go on. It won't take me long," she said, barely aware that I stood behind her. She moved on to a new spot and began to make a new mound.

"Sahaab," I protested, annoyed with myself for having asked for her help.

Then, I spotted something orange looming along the road in the distance. It was the taxi returning for me.

"Go home, will you?" I shouted at Sahaab who was still shaping mounds. She gave no hint of hearing me.

A moment later I escaped back into the taxi, thankful that the driver had returned early. I watched from the car's rear window as we rode back to Shuaiba, Sahaab's head still visible as it bobbed up and down with her frenetic movements. Then, I turned away, thrusting the sight from my mind as quickly as possible. That is when I noticed that my ring was missing from my finger. It was the ring my father had given me on my thir-

180

teenth birthday, a small red ruby eye on a serpent, the only
ring that I liked to wear. It must have slipped off from the
friction of the sand against my skin as I had dug the grave. I
resisted the sharp urge to go back to look for it, forcing myself
to look straight ahead all the way back to Shuaiba.

Some weeks later, Sameer, obviously alert to my sullen moods,
swore that he was going to borrow money from anyone who
would agree to lend him to buy me the promised MG. I let him
make his promises to me, realizing that they made him feel
good.

He had been gloomy, himself, all week. He had had an argu-
ment with one of his Kuwaiti friends and the young man had
threatened to have him thrown out of the country. It was not
the first time that Sameer had heard these words and, despite
the fact that they were not always meant to be taken seriously,
they made him even more determined to leave the country of
his own free will as soon as he could.

Until that time, however, what he actually did was buy himself something which I discovered while tidying up his room
one morning.

I usually tidied the house and his room along with my own
before school each morning as part of my chores. After I made
his bed, replaced his slippers behind the door, and removed
the empty tea glass from the table beside his bed, I sat a moment to glance at the automobile magazines filled with photo-
graphs of the latest model cars that were stashed beneath his
bed.

As I reached under the bed to return the magazines, my
fingers hit against something hard. I pulled it out, drawing my
fingers away the minute I saw it. It was a small, black pistol.

"Don't touch it."

I turned around.

Sameer stood behind me, just out of the shower. A large

towel was wrapped about his waist below his broad, hairless chest. I suddenly felt a rush of love—as though for a baby—for him. This was my brother! But the tenderness and pity for this broken brother of mine quickly washed away with a swell of contempt.

"Is it real?" I asked.

"Of course," he said, pushing me aside to pick it up.

"Where did you get it?"

"I bought it."

"When?" I said, my face frozen. "Why?"

He slipped the gun into the pages of one of the magazines which he slipped back under the bed. "To go hunting."

"Hunting? That's not a hunting gun. Anyway, since when do you hunt?"

"I'm going with friends. To Khafje."

"Some friends you must have," I said, wondering what sort of hunters used pistols to kill rabbits and gazelles. I wondered whether he intended to intimidate any of the men who had humiliated him with their threats.

"You better be careful, Sameer," I said, as I walked past him out of the room.

"Laila," he said.

I stopped, but did not turn around.

"Don't tell anybody about the gun. I might need it—if someone tries to stop us from leaving."

"Who's going to stop us?" I said, bitterness rising in me at how desperate he and I had become to leave our family. "Anyway," I said, angrily, "maybe I won't want to leave."

There was a hush that suddenly both enveloped us and separated us from each other.

Then his voice came, slow and soft. "I'll kill you if you don't."

ISABEL

26

As if worrying about meeting Saqr was not enough to think about for the moment, the next morning on the way to school Sahaab pressed something flat and shiny into my hand. It was a photograph—a black and white and slightly blurred picture of a nude woman.

At first, I simply stared. The woman was lying on her side, her right cheek resting on her palm. Her thigh was drawn up, languorously rather than modestly, and seemed disproportionately large compared to the rest of the body. The black tresses tumbling about the woman's face reached just below her shoulders and were touching in their inability to protect her bare breasts from the camera.

Yet there was nothing timid about the face, the haughty chin, the narrowing eyes. The body was rounder in the photograph, however, and riper than I would have expected. It was the smile, though, that was unsettling, the taunting curve of the mouth and its very nonchalance at the body's naked vulnerability that made my own body go numb.

Of course, it was Laila.

"Where did you find this?" I said, trying to sound as disinterested as if I were handed such a photograph every day.

"She gave it to me."

I felt my mouth fall open. "What?"

Sahaab's lip started to quiver but her eyes lit up with the triumphant satisfaction of knowing something that I did not, of having me at her mercy. "We got into a fight. I told her she was acting crazy, that she was being nasty to everyone, that missing classes would get her into trouble—I was trying to help her. She started to shout at me and told me I didn't know anything, that if I thought that being rude was bad, I should see what else she could do. Then, she showed it to me."

"I don't believe you," I said. "Maybe it's not her. It's not even clear who it is."

"She said it was her," Sahaab said, now looking offended, almost sad, that I did not believe her.

"Others saw this?"

"I don't think so. I hid it. She didn't seem to care if they did."

I drew in a breath, hating to share with Sahaab such an intimate, embarrassing thing about Laila. "Why didn't you give it back to her?"

"I was afraid to. You know how she can get. I haven't shown it to anyone but you."

I glared at Sahaab, warning her that I expected her to keep silent about this. I was annoyed at her for aggravating an already overwhelming morning. "Well, what do you expect me to do?"

She shrugged.

"Let me think about it," I said, as I stuck the picture deep into my mathematics book.

The picture seemed to weigh a ton, making me feel as guilty as if it were a bag of stolen money.

186

"Isabel?" Sahaab said when we reached the school and I hurried through the gate ahead of her to be alone.

"What?"

"I'm ashamed for Laila. Are you?"

I glanced back at Sahaab's docile face, at her drooping, gray eyes.

"No," I said, hoping that my face was not as flushed as it felt. "No, I'm not."

"So?" Laila said, when I showed her the picture.

Just as I expected, she made no attempt to take it from me or to hurry and rattle off some explanation. It was, rather, as though she were relieved to have been found out.

"Who took it?" I demanded.

"Why do you want to know?"

We were walking down the hall, past the row of water fountains. She stopped to get a drink, dawdling over the fountain as though hoping that I would go on to class ahead of her. As I watched her bend over the fountain, I remembered the roundness of the flesh in the picture. My mind screamed. I felt weak.

"Why did you do it?" I asked, unable to force calm into my voice.

She stood, licking the water that trickled down her chin. "Because I wanted to."

"But, why? Aren't you ashamed?"

"There's no shame in love," she said.

"This isn't *love*," I said, flinging the picture onto the speckled tile.

She shrugged. "I need money."

"You got paid for this?"

"This and others."

I could not believe what I heard. "What do you need money for?"

"I want to leave."

"To leave? Leave here?"

187

"I want to go back to Lebanon," she said, so softly that I barely heard.

"Leave home? What about your family? You love your family—your mother—"

"I don't love them—I don't love any of them. I hate this place!"

I was suddenly shaken. I loved Kuwait. I loved the desert. I could not conceive of not loving the only place I knew. Even on our visits back to New York every few years I could not wait to get back to my beloved compound which was home to me. Yet, I knew how difficult it must have been for Laila to grow up with her family, with her sour-faced brother, her fluffy, naive mother, her distant father. Yet, I did not want her to leave them—did not want her to leave *me*.

She said nothing, and I guessed that she knew what I was thinking as she casually stooped to retrieve the picture from the floor and slipped it into her pocket.

"I thought you were happy," I pressed on. "You say that Sameer is going to buy you a car. What about that?"

When she still said nothing, I felt the anger rise in my throat. "Who took these pictures?" I demanded, knowing that I had to get to the bottom of this.

She simply stared at me, as though she did not know the answer.

For a second, a thought crossed my mind. It seemed absurd, and yet I could not rid myself of wondering if she was drugged in some way. We occasionally heard rumors of drugs such as hashish used at expatriate teen parties. None of us at the Fahaheel school had any first-hand knowledge of drugs but I remembered Andrea's stories of alcohol and drug parties in England and I wondered whether Laila had taken any of it. With an older brother who came and went as he pleased, who might have had access to drugs, she might have tried them. I remembered Andrea's story of being at Saqr's Tower and being served beer, of the fumbling American boy who had drunkenly wandered into the women's quarters. Sameer had been to these parties, he had once told Laila. Perhaps he had taken her. Perhaps she had been drugged and photographed. There were all sorts of lurid tales in the women's magazines of women being entrapped like this in Cairo or Beirut, but it hardly seemed a thing that would happen to anyone I knew.

"Do I know the person who took these?" I asked.

She lifted her eyebrows, perhaps surprised by my persistence, and gave a light nod.

Finally I blurted it out. "Was it Saqr who took this picture?"

Without a moment's hesitation, perhaps simply to shut me up, she flashed those spirited slate eyes and retorted, "Maybe it was."

27

Shortly before five, as Saqr had instructed, I rode south along the beach beyond the compound fence. Noor was unusually frisky that afternoon, bounding over the sand like a filly, her head searching the air as her hooves splashed in the shallow water.

It was an extraordinary day, two days away from December and cool, filled with the settled colors of Autumn—the yellow-aqua of the Gulf, the mauve sky, the white sand. Sea gulls dipped into the rippling water and soared up again, their shrill cawing echoing above us. I reined in Noor, guiding her around the large spheres of lavender jellyfish that had been washed ashore, their pink middles still glowing with life.

Unlike the flat, groomed beaches of our compound, the shore beyond the barbed-wire fence was hilly and wild and reeked of seaweed and decomposing fish. It was littered with dead crabs and sea cucumbers as well as assorted garbage that had washed ashore from the oil tankers. Occasionally, there were the black remains of a fire from somebody's picnic the Friday before.

I slipped off of Noor's back and walked beside her for a while, leading her after me as I bent to inspect shells, trying to divert my mind from Saqr. By now, however, I knew all of the sea debris from my years of walking along this shore and it was hard to find anything new enough to engage my imagination.

As usual on an afternoon in the middle of the week, the beach was deserted. I remembered the afternoon when I rode along this same spot as a child with my father and discovered the Tower for the first time. That day now seemed more remote than a fairy tale, although except for several tin-roof beach shelters erected by the government for picnickers, the beach had hardly changed.

I scanned the ridges that rose sharply from the shore for a sign of Saqr driving down from the main road. In my mind, I tried to draw his features—his eyes that were narrow, unlike most Arabs', his cleft chin, his hooked nose. It had been a long time since I had seen him and I was surprised to find that I could not form a clear picture of his face.

At 6:15 I was still alone on the beach, feeling foolish for agreeing to the meeting in such vague terms. For all I knew, Saqr might have meant some other spot entirely, or he may have simply been testing me to see whether or not I would actually show up, the way that Laila sometimes teased me to do something daring.

Then, suddenly, I noticed a distant, buzzing noise from the sea. Rounding the bend on the water against the horizon was a small burst of white. It was a speedboat cutting across the water like a renegade whitecap. It reached a point straight out in front of me, then sharply turned inland and approached the shore in a spew of froth like a great white fish.

In an instant, Saqr was out of the boat. Bare-chested, his

191

trousers rolled up to his calves, he leaped across the sand like some wild Sindbad.

He stopped right in front of me. "You came," he said, panting.

I started to giggle. Boyishly disheveled, he seemed vulnerable in a way I had never seen. "I came."

He had grown a mustache since I last saw him, but his smooth brown cheek and grin had not changed a bit. "Hello," he said. The expanse of his chest was so inviting that I looked away. He reached for Noor's reins. "So, this is the famous horse."

"This is Noor," I said, remembering that I had told him about her.

He stroked her nose and neck, uttering strange, guttural sounds. Usually skittish with strangers, Noor did not seem to mind Saqr's touch.

"You must like horses," I said.

"I have three," he said, patting Noor's neck.

"Do you ride often?"

"When I go hunting."

"I thought most hunting was done in Jeeps these days."

He smiled. "I hunt with a falcon and a horse," he said, perhaps remembering that I once ridiculed the new so-called hunting with modern vehicles and rifles.

"Where do you hunt?"

"South."

He did not need to say more. Anyone who lived in Kuwait knew that 'south' referred to a section of the desert supposedly abounding in gazelles and wild rabbits and a sort of private sporting grounds—for the Sheikhs and their friends. A bin Ahmad would have had no trouble hunting there.

The three of us—Saqr, I, the horse—stood still as the waves made light, rhythmic advances toward us.

Then, Saqr reached out and touched my hair that suddenly seemed as tangled as the seaweed at our feet from the salt air and my ride over. His fingers moved lightly, yet his touch was strong and confident, that of someone accustomed to doing whatever he wanted.

He moved closer until his face was just above mine. I felt my eyes absorb his eyes, absorb his lashes, his black eyebrows that slowly lifted as though in question. I took a deep breath and closed my eyes, reaching out to him, clinging to him for balance and assurance that he was real.

I felt his lips the way I had in his car in a warm, long kiss. This time, I kissed him back, drawing in his lips as he did mine, tasting the salt of the sea on them. I caressed his straight, coarse hair, and he pushed against me until I suddenly grew aware of something hard against my belly. So, this was what was said to happen to men when they were aroused! I was shocked, then elated to have caused this to happen to Saqr. But then, I drew back.

"Saqr, is there anyone else? Is it true that you have another girlfriend?"

He looked dazed. "Where did you hear that?"

"Is it true?" I put up my hands to stop him from touching me, further.

"No. Of course it's not true."

"I don't believe you."

"Why did you come then?"

Suddenly, without warning, he lowered his head and kissed me, again, hard. Startled, I brought my fingers to my mouth.

"Why did you come?" he repeated.

"You asked me to."

"Why did you really come?"

"What do you mean?"

"On the telephone you sounded as though you wouldn't."

I was sure, now, that I had made a mistake in coming. Perhaps he was the sort of man who loved a woman so long as she was unattainable. He was a hunter. I had made myself accessible prey.

I moved further away from him and turned to the water,

193

wishing that things were not so complicated, that I could simply tell him how much I loved him and not have to worry about losing him.

"Would you like to take a spin?" he said, suddenly.

I realized that I had been staring at the sleek, white boat as it bobbed and dodged its own silvery reflection from where Saqr had anchored it in the water.

"What will I do with Noor?"

"We'll tie her to this," he said, dragging up a heavy piece of driftwood.

"I don't think she'll stay. I never leave her unattended."

"She'll stay," he said, tying her reins to the wood, speaking a few more husky words to her. He beckoned me towards the water.

The wind whipped our hair, filling my lungs as though I would burst. We laughed, skimming the cobalt water, the hull of the boat thudding against the swells. Behind me, through the dusk, I could just make out the flare of our refinery and compound with its myriad twinkling lights that were beginning to shine. Ahead of us, along the coast, several more flares from distant oil fields were becoming discernible.

The sea was opaque, now, dark and sullen. Saqr steered with one hand and held me with his other arm, maneuvering deftly around the swells. I leaned into him, pressing my cheek into his shoulder, closing my eyes to the quenching spray. The roar of the deafening motors and the boat's rhythmic, sharp slaps against the water were hypnotic. I had never felt this free before, nor this happy. I wanted to stretch this moment of being wrapped in his arm, his warm skin against mine, into a decade.

For the first time, I began to hate a woman I did not even know—a Kuwaiti woman from his own clan—who would one day claim him. I could not bear to think that someone else would one day have him for herself, and yet I understood too well that he would not be allowed to love me. Even now, snuggled against him in the boat with nobody else in sight, I felt that we were being pried apart. In the end, as Laila had said, we would be separated by his family and by his own inability to oppose their wishes. I stared at his face. His smile was that of one who was used to being watched and who enjoyed it. I wanted to keep that image of him forever, his youth, his disarray, eating life as though it were his to feast upon.

For a brief moment I wished that Laila could see me enjoying a man's touch the way she had tirelessly assured me I one day would. I even imagined her standing in my place, receiving Saqr's caresses, gulping in the sea and air and reveling in the sheer bliss of it all. It was only a flicker of a thought, however, for we were just rounding the last, jutting bend of the shore line that would bring us in full view of the Tower.

The Tower of Dreams.

It was my father's voice in my ears rather than Saqr's, once again explaining the lone, seaside fortress to me, its ramparts and turrets. I shuddered now as I had shuddered that day as a little girl to hear of the one-time slave station, that bastion of power and sadness.

It seemed smaller seen from the sea this way, though it still glowered from the incline overlooking the beach. There was a dimly lit window at the top and some sort of flag crowning the wind tower. The walls, still partly crumbled, were illuminated by an array of shimmering, white-bellied sea gulls that calmly perched in a straight line as though at attention.

Saqr shifted gears, steering the boat into the shallow water.

On the shore, a figure appeared as though awaiting our approach.

I reached for Saqr's arm.

"Who is that?"

"He works for me."

"I don't want to go," I said.

"Just for a little while," he said, advancing toward the dark shore.

I shook his arm. "I want to go back."

"You wanted to come, to see the tower," he said, sounding surprised and hurt.

"I did...only I'm not ready, yet. Please take me back."

"But we're already here. At least come in and have a look."

Suddenly, as if she were right there before me, I saw Laila—Laila of the nude photograph—supple and surrendering, challenging.

"I promise—I'll come some other time."

"When?" His voice seemed angry, detached, as though he were not really beside me but all around me. I glanced at the figure standing on the beach. I felt exposed.

"Next week. I'll come again next week."

Saqr looked at his watch, as though wondering whether he had missed an appointment, then looked back at me. I had, clearly, made him unhappy. But, then, all alone out here I was still completely at his mercy. He could force me to do anything he wanted.

Yet I was not really frightened, for that was not Saqr. He probably had never had to fight for a girl in his life and it would not have occurred to him to use his strength against me like that. Getting me to agree to go to the Tower with him was the most forcing he would ever do.

He pushed the gear forward and jolted us back and away from the Tower in a sweeping crescent.

Once again, the water parted before us and we left a trail of froth in our wake. The boat dropped hard against the swells that Saqr, this time, made no attempt to avoid.

I stood beside him as I had done on the way over, my blouse plastered against my chest, but this time I clutched the windshield instead of his arm, ashamed for being frightened, for holding back. I wanted him to speak to me, to touch me or try to talk me into going back to the Tower. But he remained silent and kept his hands on the steering wheel.

Finally, we neared the place where we had left Noor. I

scanned the beach for a sign of her but what I spotted in the darkness on the shore, instead, were *two* horses. My heart froze. On one of the horses sat a rider.

Saqr's face showed no emotion at the sight of the man on the horse, neither curiosity nor alarm. He remained in the boat a few feet out in the water while I slid out and waded ashore.

The man on the horse was, of course, my father. Since he had no way of knowing who Saqr was I fabricated a somewhat convincing story of a chance meeting with a brother of a friend who had happened to pass by in his boat. But as we rode home together in the dark, my father's anger loomed heavy between us. I knew that he must have been cold with fear to have discovered Noor alone on the beach. I listened, quietly, as he told me that I had behaved irresponsibly, that I would be confined to the house after school for the next two weeks.

28

Five months later, I stood at a mirror in the long, rectangular school bathroom brushing out my hair. I had been let out of class early to deliver a message to the Headmistress and then had gone straight to the bathroom to get ready for our final rehearsal for the graduation ceremony. The school bathrooms in Fahaheel were spacious and air-conditioned and filled with enough mirrors to accommodate teenage girls. Yet, whenever I walked into them, I could not help remembering the narrow bathrooms of our Shuaiba school where many of my friends had had to sit at one time or another with their lice-infested hair wrapped in nets. I could still sense the fumes of the dreaded DDT whenever I walked into these bathrooms, half-expecting to find a girl crouched in a corner, her hair soaked in the whitish disinfectant, sobbing.

The Headmistress had asked for a final dress rehearsal for the graduation celebration that was to take place in two days. Dressed in traditional, gold-embroidered Kuwaiti gowns, we were to file into the dining hall accompanied by the music teacher on the accordion and sit in rows of ten in front of the stage while the Headmistress addressed the audience of mothers and teachers. Laila and I were among the girls to receive awards for scholastic accomplishments and we were to sit at the end of the first row in order to go up to the stage to shake the Headmistress's hand.

When each girl had received her graduation certificate, the entire class would walk up to the stage to sing the national anthem and then perform a Kuwaiti women's dance commemorating the days of old Kuwait—a song about the pearl fishing season when divers used to be away at sea for months at a time in search of the oysters which yielded the famed Kuwaiti pearls. As we danced, we would lift our glittering, outer gowns to accentuate our movements, then toss our heads forward and down so that our hair nearly swept the floor. I had loved this dance ever since I had first watched the older girls perform it at the Shuaiba school while I was still in the first grade. Now, it was our turn to perform it at our own graduation. After the dance, we were to leave the stage and join our mothers and teachers in the next room for refreshments.

The bell rang.

Other girls rushed into the bathroom, yanking out the elastic that held their hair in ponytails or braids. They pulled iridescent chiffon gowns out of school bags and slipped them on over uniforms. We were to graduate in these native *nashels*, with our hair loose, like brides. Non-Kuwaiti girls had to have *nashels* made especially for the occasion. My gown was a deep green. Laila's was red.

Sahaab came over to me as we dressed. Her new pink gown, warm against her pallid cheeks, had been made too long for her.

"Can't you pin it up?" I said, annoyed that she could have

overlooked this. "You might stumble getting onto the stage."

Then, as usual, hating myself for being harsh with her, I knelt and pinned it up, myself. For although Sahaab, like the rest of us, seemed glad enough to be finished with school, I knew that her education would end with this graduation. Rather than send her on to the new women's university that had just opened in Kuwait, her father, to ease his financial burden, would probably marry her off in the coming months, ending any freedom that she might have.

"Where's Laila?" I asked.

"In the infirmary," she said.

"Why?" I tried not to show the worry that would seize me, lately, whenever anyone referred to Laila's erratic behavior.

"Her usual headache."

"She'll miss rehearsal," I said, resenting Sahaab's sarcastic tone, even though Laila's frequent claims to headaches were beginning to exasperate everyone. Even the teachers assumed it was a simply a ruse to get out of class.

The bathroom was quickly filling with the sweet scent of the coconut oil that the girls had rubbed into their hair to make it shine. It was beginning to flutter with color as they swept kohl wands across their dark eyes to outline them and smoothed bright red lipstick onto their lips.

Things were quite different from when we had first started school. There were only several of us left from the original Shuaiba first grade. There were practically no girls who still lived in straw shacks or in mud-brick houses with wind-towers as there had been when we first came to Kuwait; even modest families now lived in apartment buildings or in modern houses. Everyone had telephones and televisions and many girls had cars with drivers who drove them to and from school rather than ride the buses. In little more than ten years there seemed to have been a hundred years worth of changes.

As I watched my friends, I thought of Saqr. Their every gesture and feature suddenly reminded me of him—the way that

Ruquiya's thick hair flowed up and back from her forehead like his did, the rich, brown color of Dana's face and hands like his.

I had not seen him since that November afternoon, months ago, when we had ridden in his boat. He had not called me after that and I had not gone to the Tower again, as I had promised, because I had not been allowed to ride for several weeks after being discovered with him on the beach. Saqr had obviously gone back to England afterwards and he had not contacted me during the spring vacation.

Yet rather than forget him, my longing for him had grown steadily stronger. I tirelessly dreamed up scenarios in which I would express my love to him, not caring whether or not we had a future together. I wanted him—if only for a few weeks or months—and no longer cared what he might think of me. I blamed myself over and over for my cowardice, for not having gone all the way to the Tower with him as he had wanted that evening. If only I could have, for once, let myself go!

As we began to line up outside the dining room, several of my friends reached out and touched my hair, gently, more out of fondness than curiosity. Although my hair was now as coarse as theirs from the hard water and as rippled from being braided, it was altogether different. Even after knowing me all these years they still seemed struck by its color. They sometimes asked to brush it out, to watch the static lift it, hat-like, about my head. Sometimes they rubbed oil into it as they did theirs, to make it behave. Yet, what they could not know was how much I wanted to be like *them*, to have hair that was so black it shone blue in the light, to dissolve into their dark skin and look out from their wide, settled eyes, to become one of them. *To be like Saqr.* Whenever I looked in the mirror and found the same green crystals for eyes, my same light eyebrows and red hair that I had hated all of my life, I wanted to cry.

As we stood outside the dining hall, our hair fanned across a brilliant sea of twinkling chiffon, Laila walked past us, heading for the bathroom.

201

I left the line and ran in after her.

"I was going to look for you," I said, pausing at the doorway, stunned by her disheveled appearance. Her face was as pale as a lemon.

"I'll be out in a minute," she said.

"What's wrong?" I asked.

She stood at the mirror as we had done earlier, ripping the elastic from her hair. I suddenly realized how tired she looked, a little stooped as though she had lost weight. I thought of how she had talked lately of having had enough of school, enough of trying to fit into a family in which she did not belong, enough of living in the desert. She had spoken of going back to Lebanon, of her body no longer tolerating the endless heat.

She washed her face, then she filled her hands with water and doused her arms. She lifted her right foot into the sink and started washing it.

"What are you doing?"

"I'm washing."

"I can see that," I said, "but we'll be late if we don't go now. We're all supposed to walk in together."

"You go on. I'll be there in a minute," she said.

"What are you washing for?"

"I'm going to pray," she said, simply.

"Now?"

"Yes." She put down her wet foot and lifted up the other.

"Can't you wait until we finish?"

"No. You go ahead. I'll catch up."

I left just as she tied a scarf about her head, tucking in the traces of hair at her face, to begin the prayer.

When she did get to the dining hall, radiant in her red *nashel*, the Headmistress was signaling for those girls who were to receive awards to proceed toward the stage. I pulled Laila into line behind me, as the teachers turned to look at her, looks of admonition for her tardiness plainly on their faces. But she ignored them, staring straight ahead as though fascinated by something on the stage. The red gown burned like a flame against her white skin and her eyes were more lucid than I had seen them in a long time. She seemed transformed, somehow. Like someone who had just seen a ghost.

29

Now, a week past graduation, my worries are gone. Laila is behaving more like her old ebullient, wisecracking self again. And Saqr has called me, having returned from England for the summer. I am to go to the Tower to see him. I can barely think of his body against mine without wilting, yet am satisfied in a small way that I have made him wait until I am ready.

We have set the time and place where we will meet—the Tower, 8:30, the first of June.

This time, Laila will be the one to take me, for she now has her new car. Where it not for her, I might never have been able to fully appreciate this occasion. Had she not coached me all those years, carefully stripping away the petals of my ignorance, I might still be as hopeless as Sahaab or some of the other girls who graduated with us yet have never savored the thrill of love.

Yet, there is another reason that I have asked Laila to accompany me. A selfish one. For I want to see her and Saqr meet, again, to see for myself once and for all whether anything had ever happened between them.

As I wait for Laila to come, annoyed that she is late, yet too happy to be anything but grateful to her, I feel like a child again, waiting for my mother to put me into one of her stories of perilous adventure, waiting for my father to show me what he has promised will be the biggest sand box that I will ever see...

30

Voices float about the room, beating about my head like locusts, like sand. My forehead throbs. From some place beyond, some place within my heavy head, comes a ringing followed by the familiar, distant voice of my mother.

"No," I hear her say, "she hasn't awakened yet. Yes, yes I'll let you know. Yes, she'll be all right. It's just the shock. She's been sedated." I feel myself sinking, being pulled away from her voice. I try to open my mouth.

Then, later, I hear her say, "Come in. She's still asleep. Sit down."

For a moment, I wonder whether I am nine years old again and still lying in the hospital after my riding accident. Then I see my clothes, my dress and shoes, on a chair in the corner of my bedroom. I remember. I am going to the Tower. I am waiting for Laila.

It is dark outside my windows. There seem to be more voices now, light, pattering, female voices drifting in from the living room. I am a child again, listening to my parents and their friends talking as though from some remote place where they cannot be reached. I try to call them, to scream, but I cannot open my mouth.

I think I recognize Sahaab's mother's slow, distracted words. No, it is in English. It is the voice of our neighbor, Andrea Deer's mother. They are Mrs. Deer's British syllables, low and erect.

"I suppose it's not surprising," she says.

"Why do you say that?" says my mother. Her voice is deeper than usual, husky.

"Because of the way they regard women here," the other voice says.

"How do they regard them?"

All at once I know that I am not supposed to be lying in bed. I have to get dressed. I must go to the Tower!

"Women mean nothing here. Like cats. Totally insignificant."

"That's not true," my mother says, her voice tired, tired of having to always explain away the misconceptions of her expatriate friends. "Anyway, that has nothing to do with it."

The other voice returns, lower and slightly apologetic this time. "I mean, for a brother to kill his sister like that just because he suspects her of being interested in some boy ... like any normal girl."

Kill. The word seems to split, to explode into a million fragments. I try to move my legs, to get up, but they seem buried in the bed.

"It's not necessarily normal here," my mother says.

"Still, is that any reason to kill her? Your own sister? Your own flesh and blood?" The woman sounds upset, her voice rising, shredding itself into two voices that fly side by side.

I start to remember again. I have been waiting for Laila. We are going to the Tower together. She has promised to take me but she has made me wait—my parents are playing cards—

Then there is the telephone call. I run and answer it, but it is not Laila. I call my father away from the card table—

"That wasn't the reason," my mother is saying.

"Why did he do it then?"

I hear whispers. I try to lift my head to listen, forcing it a fraction off the pillow.

I suddenly remember my father's face as he answered the telephone. I hear my own screaming when he told me the news.

Mrs. Deer's voice cuts through the whispers. "My God! How do you know?"

When my mother speaks, I cannot believe her words.

"My God!" There is a pause. I imagine Mrs. Deer's plump, rosy cheeks drained of life. "Was he jealous?"

This time, I cannot hear my mother's answer.

"Was he crazy?" Mrs. Deer sounds hysterical. "Do you know the family."

"Yes," my mother says, calmly. "I know the family.

I drop my head back onto the pillow. I try to understand what I have just heard. I remember waiting at the door before the telephone rang. I was too happy to be sad, then, too happy to think of Laila or of Sameer or of anyone buried in the desert.

I think only of the Tower of Dreams, of driving there tonight with Laila in her red MG, of the mud walls which I will enter tonight for the first time and where, after what has seemed like an eternity, I will finally give myself to Saqr.

Epilogue

31

One night, many years later, after Kuwait has become a dream, a chapter between birth and death, a warm memory tucked into the pages of my life, I see him, again.

It is in London. I have flown in from Beirut where I am living and have been in the airport waiting for my flight from London to New York which has been delayed because of fog. Finally, it is announced that certain flights have been canceled and the passengers are to be put up for the night in a hotel near the airport.

We are driven by bus to the nearby hotel and as we wait in line to check in, disgruntled and tired, I spot him.

I do not realize that it is him, at first, only that I am drawn to his face. My eyes race across his features like fingertips across braille. He is tall, graying, tapping his foot impatiently.

It is only when he actually looks at me, as though my rapid breath or stark gaze has alerted him, when he, too, seems unable to look away, that I feel myself blush in recognition.

Almost too soon, for I have not yet adjusted to the shock, he comes over to me. "Is it Isabel?"

I almost wish that it was not really him standing before me looking first at me, then at the girl with the brown hair who stands beside me, already as tall as I, and who now unabashedly stares back at him.

"My daughter," I say, without removing my eyes from his face, wondering how I have changed for him and wondering whether he can sense the wrenching quiver that he has sent through me.

We sit in the lobby and order coffee while my daughter goes to gaze at the dark windows of the closed hotel shops.

"How old is she?" he says.

"Fourteen," I say, without hesitating. She is the age that I was when I had first met him.

He stares at her a few moments. "She doesn't have your red hair," he says, as though trying to picture the father who has given her the dark hair.

"No, she doesn't."

As we talk, I begin to recognize the Saqr I once knew. His face is fuller, his hawk's nose fleshier, but his eyes are still sharp, still pierce intensely when he fixes them on me. His demeanor still radiates an undeniable presence—a dinosaur, I had thought of, then. Yet now I see that he is more like a leopard, implying strength tempered with a sensual elegance. I realize, a little surprised, that he is not—has never been—a beautiful man, not even a handsome man in the usual sense. What I must have found so mesmerizing then, as I do even now, was the consuming reflection of warmth, the full passion of the desert that still reverberates off his body like a mirror.

He still retains the easy grace of one born into great wealth. He tells me that he has married his cousin, that he has five children, all in Kuwait. He is traveling to Paris on business.

"Have you been back since—you left?" he says.

"No. I've never wanted to go back."

212

He looks surprised, perhaps even hurt.

"I didn't want to see all the changes. It will never be the same again, will it?"

He seems to ponder this. "No. We can't go back. But, you would be impressed by the new buildings, by the highways, the trees. It has grown tremendously."

My daughter returns. She wants to go up to the room to sleep. I rise to go with her, but Saqr asks me to stay.

"Only a few minutes," he says, looking at me. He orders us more coffee.

When we are alone, he asks me how long it has been since I left Kuwait. I calculate twenty years. I had gone on to the University in Beirut, had gotten married and lived there ever since. I am on my way to visit my parents who now live in New York, again.

Now it is my turn.

The first thing I ask him is whether or not his family still owns the Tower of Dreams. He looks at me, surprised, as though I have said something amusing. He laughs, softly. "Do you still remember it?"

He owns it now, he says. It is getting shabby and needs re-building. He is often tempted to tear it down completely.

He must see my lips tremble when he says this. I am thinking of those afternoon rides with my father, of coming around the bend in the hush of a desolate beach to find the crumbling mud walls, the turrets and wind-tower waiting there for us, sweeping up from the sand almost without beginning or end.

I see myself beside him in the boat that afternoon, the salt wind matting our hair and skin, the bow hammering against the rising swells of the silent, black sea as we race toward the Tower, and toward a fate that would never be. Then, I think of that later time, the time when I had promised to meet him there, when I had waited, endlessly, for Laila to come and pick me up in her new MG.

What had I intended to do that evening? I still wonder. Would my life have been different, today, had Laila shown up as planned to take me to Saqr?

Saqr tells me, now, that the only thing that stops him from destroying the old Tower is a memory. The memory of a girl has kept it intact all these years, kept his youth intact within its walls along with the memory that the girl had promised to come to him.

We stare at each other, suddenly losing our former awkwardness, suddenly closer than we have ever been. Safe in our separate lives, the years have suddenly freed us.

"I had meant to come that night," I say, quietly.

"Did you?"

"I was supposed to come with Laila—"

I stop. It has been years since I have spoken of her to anyone. I do not want to talk about her, now, not with Saqr. Nor do I want to talk about Sameer. A picture of him—handcuffed and flanked by police—had filled the Kuwait newspapers and magazines for weeks afterward. I do not even want to know what became of him, whether he had been imprisoned or simply executed for killing his sister. I have cultivated a careful indifference, a numbness, towards Laila since that night.

My mother had flown with me to Beirut a week later to see that I recuperate in a summer camp in the cool mountains of Lebanon, away from Kuwait. By October, when she had judged me recovered enough to start college, she had returned to Kuwait alone, leaving me in the safety of a campus dorm where I had always envisioned being with Laila, who had already been granted a scholarship.

Only in an occasional dream did Laila invade my life any more, almost as though to purposely haunt me, to wring free in sleep the tears that left my pillow wet in the morning. I wake with that eternal question on my lips that I demand an answer for—why had she chosen to give up, chosen death, when she had been more alive than any of us? Sometimes I would even replay my mother's voice as I had heard her trying to explain the tragedy to Mrs. Deer that evening when I had been barely conscious from being sedated:

"He was her lover," my mother's voice had said.

"Her brother?"

"Yes."

"You mean, her brother killed her because he was her lover?"

"Yes."

"My God! How did you know? Did he confess?"

"He took them to the desert where he buried her," my mother said.

"My God!"

Although Saqr would undoubtedly know what had become of Sameer, for a tragedy of that nature in Kuwait would be remembered for decades, I do not want an update.

Finally, after midnight, we rise to go to our rooms. We are taking different flights in the morning. He is going to Paris, I to America. It seems absurd that we have both been detained on this particular night in London. And yet, it is almost as though it were planned.

We ride up together in the elevator. His room is on the seventh floor. Mine is on the ninth. He smiles at me, polite and restrained, and I cannot help wondering whether he wants me to go to his room with him.

I suddenly smell the sea again, feel Noor's coarse mane lash at my face as her hoofs scatter wet sand. I feel the softness of Saqr's lips on mine, feel myself cling to him. I want to hold him a last time, tonight, to show him how much I have wanted to be his woman all these years.

When I think of the woman who is his wife, now, it is not with envy but rather with the knowledge that there is a part of him that she will never know. I think of her with a rush of pity.

The elevator stops at the seventh floor. The door opens. Saqr hesitates a moment. I sense that he expects me to accompany him, perhaps just to talk about the old Kuwait. But he does not insist. It is not his way.

An abrupt spasm of fear rips through me as I realize that I might never see him again. A coincidence like this only happens once. I feel lost, suddenly, seized by a desperate need to leave him with something that will remain with him.

"Please," I whisper, quickly, feeling as though I will suffocate, "Saqr, please don't destroy the Tower."

His eyebrows suddenly lift as though I am fourteen again and have just said the funniest thing in the world. He smiles. My heart races. For a sliver of a second I see Laila's face, sense that tenuous thread knotting me to her, to my childhood, to Saqr, about to snap.

Saqr pauses a moment, then steps out into the hall and turns to face me. His eyes soften. He knows that a part of me has already gone to him, is calling to the rest of me to follow and live all that I have longed for all these years. Once again, I smell the dank, salt air of the playground in Shuaiba as we stroll arm in arm chanting the day's lessons, I cling to the older girl who, on my first day, shows me off to the other girls and teachers; I gaze across the dining hall table through the delicious scent of lentils and cumin at the fathomless black eyes of a beautiful, headstrong girl named Laila.

Then, although I know that I will regret it later, that I will never forgive myself for not reclaiming that part of myself that Saqr is offering me now, I let the elevator door close between us, let it close out all the memories and yearnings, and allow it to carry me upward, forever, as though into a dream.

Kathryn K. Abdul-Baki was born in Washington, D.C. She grew up in Iran, Kuwait, Beirut, and Jerusalem where she attended Arabic, British, and American schools. She attended the American University of Beirut, Lebanon, and earned a B.A. in journalism from George Washington University in Washington, D.C. She has an M.A. in creative writing from George Mason University, Virginia.

Ms. Abdul-Baki worked as a journalist and features-writer for an English weekly newspaper in Bahrain before devoting her time to writing fiction. Her works include a collection of short stories, *Fields of Fig and Olive: Ameera and Other Stories of the Middle East*, also published by Three Continents Press, and *Ghost Songs*, a family saga set in modern Jerusalem.

She received the Mary Roberts Rinehart award for short fiction in 1984. She currently resides in McLean, Virginia with her husband and three children.